"Why did you pretend to be in love with me?"

Courtney's voice was raw with pain. "Did you derive some sort of sick pleasure from humiliating me? I would have given you what you were after. All you had to do was ask!"

Jonas's mouth had thinned into a white line of anger. "If I wasn't in love with you, then do you mind telling me what you think I wanted?"

"You wanted clout with the tribe. As my supposed fiancé, you thought you'd have more credibility with the tribal elders."

There was a sharp intake of breath. "That's fascinating. But the fact is, Chief Bob Willie doesn't approve of your life-style, Courtney. The chief's a traditionalist. If anything, being involved with you has caused me to lose face with him."

D0032163

Rebecca Winters, an American writer and mother of four, is a graduate of the University of Utah who has also studied overseas at schools in Switzerland and France, including the Sorbonne. She is currently teaching French and Spanish to junior high school students. Despite her busy schedule, Rebecca always finds time to write. She's already researching the background for her next book for Harlequin Romance!

Books by Rebecca Winters

RITES
OF LOVE

Rebecca Winters

Harlequin Books

TORONTO • NEW YORK • LONDON
AMSTERDAM • PARIS • SYDNEY • HAMBURG
STOCKHOLM • ATHENS • TOKYO • MILAN

ISBN 0-373-03120-3

Harlequin Romance first edition April 1991

RITES OF LOVE

CHAPTER ONE

"COURTNEY?" The deep voice of a man stopped Courtney Blake in her tracks as she walked through the Miccosukee Cultural Center. *Jonas!* She couldn't believe it. She had to steady herself against the safety railing on the ramp that led to the airboat.

He'd been in Washington, D.C. working on an important tribal land transaction and wasn't supposed to be back in Miami for another week, at least! She'd been sure there was time enough to quit her job at the law firm and make preparations for her journey into the Glades before his return.

The pain of his betrayal had left her reeling and she never wanted to see or talk to him again. Did the fact that he'd cut short his business to come out to the Center mean she was still necessary in his scheme to ingratiate himself with the tribal elders? Throughout their courtship she'd foolishly believed him to be in love with her.

Waves of humiliation washed over her, but she wouldn't give him the satisfaction of knowing how his presence affected her. Schooling her features not to reveal even a hint of emotion, she turned to face him. Of medium height herself, she had to look up to take in his six-foot-plus frame, every inch of it whipcord lean.

His hair, slightly too long, was as dark as the wing of a black skimmer she could see circling in the sky. A few tendrils fell across his bronzed forehead and lifted with the slightest breeze.

"Jonas," she replied coolly, steeling herself not to be mesmerized by eyes that reflected the primordial green of the Glades surrounding them.

He slipped suntanned hands in the pockets of his loose white trousers and took a step closer. His gaze dropped to her tennis shoes, traveled slowly over her long, shapely legs in faded jeans, her full curves under the calico blouse, finally resting on the waist-length auburn braid that fell over her right shoulder. In the past, such an intimate appraisal would have propelled her straight into his arms.

"It's gratifying to know you haven't forgotten my name quite yet." His voice was taut with suppressed anger. "What's going on, Courtney? When you saw me off at the airport two weeks ago, I was under the impression that our relationship meant as much to you as it did to me. Why have you run away without a word of explanation? If you thought you could elude me, you're very much mistaken."

"No." She paused, choosing her words carefully. "I didn't think that. But I couldn't see any point in continuing our relationship. My research grant for Oklahoma came through while you were away, and since I no longer need the word processing job to make ends meet, I decided to leave."

Laura Winston, an associate in the prestigious Bal Harbour law firm owned by Jonas and his father, Silas Payne, hadn't attempted to hide her delight when Courtney tendered her resignation. In fact, she'd continually asked Courtney when she'd be quitting since she knew Courtney's job was only temporary.

As for Silas, he'd been understanding about her sudden decision to leave, though he'd expressed his regret and praised the quality of her work.

Jonas's handsome face darkened. "What on earth could have happened to make you quit your job without notice and vacate your apartment less than twenty-four hours later?"

"I've already answered that question," she said with barely disguised bitterness, remembering how easily she'd been taken in by his flattering interest. To her mortification, she'd loved him so much she hadn't understood he'd been patronizing her throughout their two-month courtship. From the very beginning, her feelings for him had been so intense, she'd been completely blind to his real motivations.

He stared at her for an uncomfortably long moment, his green eyes narrowed and watchful between their black lashes. "Don't play games with me, Courtney."

Her facial muscles tightened. "I've never played games. It's not in the Miccosukee nature." The image of a gloating Laura wishing Courtney the best of luck on her impending project in Oklahoma flashed through Courtney's mind, increasing her anger. "Now you'll have to excuse me."

But when she tried to move away, he blocked her path. A dull flush stained his cheeks. "You're not going anywhere until I have answers."

Jonas could be a frightening adversary, as those who'd faced him in a courtroom could attest, but she wasn't intimidated.

"You don't seem to understand," she said in a low voice, not wanting to attract any more attention. "There's nothing more to say. I'm no longer on the payroll."

His hands tightened into fists and a tiny vein pulsed at his temple. "After what we've shared the past few months, you don't really think I buy that do you? Or do you think I'm going to let you walk out of my life? Deny it all you want but we've experienced something rare and wonderful—something that goes beyond the physical—something I've never found with another woman, and I *know*—" his voice shook "—that you feel the same way."

"You're saying these things to the wrong woman." She turned to leave but he grabbed her arm. Involuntarily, she felt her pulse flutter like the wings of the tiny orchid butterfly hovering above them.

"What the hell is *that* supposed to mean?"

"Let go of me," she demanded, ignoring his question. "I have work to do."

"What work?"

"Running the airboat."

"You're a guide?" he asked incredulously, his grip tightening in full view of the tourists. "I thought you didn't need another job."

"I don't", she said, striving to remain calm. "I'm helping a friend. Now please let me go."

"You're not a convincing liar, Courtney. I happen to know you'd depleted most, if not all, of your savings before I left for Washington, yet you refused my offer of a loan." His sensuous mouth curved with contempt. "Do you expect me to believe this type of work offers you the kind of salary you were paid at the firm?"

She took a deep breath. "I suppose being born wealthy makes you see everything in terms of money." Her voice was scornful.

"You can't live without it, Courtney. This tourist trap couldn't possibly net you more than a thousand dollars a season."

"I've already told you money has nothing to do with my taking over Henry's job for a few days. But for your information, this *tourist trap* helps sustain the lives of several dozen Indians. However, I realize that to you such a consideration must be negligible."

Jonas's eyes held a murderous glint as he slowly let go of her arm. She'd never seen him so angry. His silence was more ominous than any retort he might have flung at her.

Fearing his wrath, she stepped quickly past him to put distance between them, then groaned when she realized he was following directly behind her. "Forget any plans you had of escaping me," he threatened in a voice so cold it left her shaken.

To her consternation, he took his place next to an elderly couple seated on one of the white benches.

Within seconds they struck up a conversation with him, assuming he was a tourist like themselves.

Unsteadily, Courtney put her foot on the bar to lever herself into the driver's seat, all the while aware of Jonas's piercing gaze fastened on her.

She counted nine passengers in all, but could hardly think about them because of Jonas. His disturbing presence unnerved her to the point that she wondered how she'd make it through the tour. When it was over, he'd insist on a full explanation; there would be an ugly scene.

Clearing her throat, she said, "Good afternoon, ladies and gentlemen. I'm Courtney and I'll be your guide for this trip into *Pa-hay-okee* country, the Seminole word for 'River of Grass.' Though we're only on the outskirts of Everglades National Park, we'll be passing through terrain similar to that in the interior, so sit back and enjoy the ride."

Jonas's wintry smile mocked her remark. "Is it safe?" His question drew everyone's attention as he eyed some alligators lounging on the bank, looking like piles of old tires.

Courtney stiffened, acknowledging the challenge. His taunt revealed the depth of his anger and the desire to punish her. In this mood he was capable of saying or doing almost anything.

Adrenaline spurted through her veins as she broke out in a smile that encompassed all her passengers— except Jonas with his merciless stare. "We'll be moving too fast in the opposite direction so there's no cause for alarm,'' she said calmly, then started the motor.

"I understand they can swim up to thirty-five miles per hour," he goaded.

She took a deep breath. "It's true that on occasion they can reach that speed. It's also true that their massive jaws can snap shut with a pressure of a thousand pounds per square inch. However, they shy away from the sound of the propeller, so they'll avoid the area where we're traveling. Does anyone else want to ask a question about the alligators before we proceed?"

Several hands went up, including Jonas's. She dealt with various questions but pointedly refused to acknowledge his, explaining that they had to get going if they wanted see the sights before the Center closed for the day.

"Will we be in time to watch the alligator wrestling?" someone called out as the flat-bottomed airboat started to skim loudly over water that quickly changed to a carpet of vegetation.

With a flip of the switch Courtney turned on the microphone. "There'll be one more show at the end of the tour."

"Are we going to have the pleasure of watching you wrestle an alligator?" Jonas asked with a wolfish half smile, provoking a wave of chuckles from the men aboard. "It says in the brochure that some of the guides are performing."

Jonas was really baiting her now and she felt her cheeks grow hot. "It's a sport invented by the white man, actually, and two of the men from the tribe had to be trained. For your information, you're in the land of the Miccosukee Indians, traveling over ancient water routes that were once graced by canoes, each carved from a single cypress log. Keep in mind, as we pass over lilies and saw grass, that the water is only six inches deep as it creeps slowly southward toward the ocean.''

A dark brow quirked in mock salute at her smooth comeback. Apparently he'd decided to change tactics, because instead of asking more questions, he relaxed on the slatted wooden bench. But his glittering green eyes didn't move from her face as she spoke.

His unflinching stare upset her even more than his questions. Unlike the other tourists, who were marveling at the unique scenery, he seemed intent on not missing a single word of her prepared talk—or the slightest glance in his direction.

From the moment they'd met, several months before, he'd been like that, acting as if he wanted to know anything and everything about her. At first she'd thought his interest stemmed from the intense physical attraction they felt for each other.

But a later conversation revealed that he'd heard about her through a mutual friend, Rosa, the woman who managed the restaurant on the Red Mangrove Reservation. Rosa had been the best friend of Courtney's deceased Miccosukee mother, and acted as a surrogate aunt to Courtney.

It seemed that on several occasions Jonas had been out to the reservation to give legal counsel on various matters affecting the tribe. In the course of his visits, he'd become friendly with Rosa, eating all his meals at the restaurant. The older woman had told him about Courtney, the anthropologist who did fieldwork at the reservation. His curiosity about Courtney's doctoral thesis on the Miccosukee language had led him to seek her out.

They'd gravitated toward each other so naturally, she assumed he had no ulterior motives when he pressed her for details concerning her white father and Indian mother. She found herself telling him whatever he wanted to know about Miccosukee culture and tradition.

It had never occurred to her that he'd deliberately cultivated a close relationship for the express purpose of using her to gain the tribe's confidence and trust. It was Silas and Laura who, one night while Jonas was in Washington, just two weeks earlier, had driven the point home to Courtney.

"Courtney?" Silas poked his head inside the computer room. "Stop what you're doing and come to my office for a celebration drink. We just heard that Jonas won his case! Of course, there's still a lot to tie up and he won't be back for at least another week, but Laura and I are too excited to do any more work tonight!"

Thrilled that the Miccosukee land claim case, which had gone on for almost two years and been so important to Jonas—and to her—was finally settled, Courtney eagerly complied with Silas's invitation. Later, when Jonas called her at the apartment, she'd be able to offer her congratulations in private. The phone was her only link with Jonas right now, and she lived for his nightly calls.

Silas's office was crowded with junior attorneys and secretaries as Courtney stepped inside, but he sought her out and handed her a glass of champagne. After gaining everyone's attention he said, "I want the staff to know how much we appreciate Courtney's contribution in all this."

Courtney's bewilderment must have shown because Laura swept across the room and approached Courtney. "You know," she drawled in a pseudo-confiding tone Courtney found distasteful, "being part Miccosukee has made you the perfect resource for Jonas. It was our lucky day when the temporary services agency sent you over for an interview."

"Hear, hear," Silas interjected warmly.

"Befriending the tribe has been one of his pet projects and it'll stand him in good stead when he runs for governor," Laura explained. "It's gratifying to know you'll be part of that support group, Courtney."

Silas nodded at her statement and threw an affectionate arm around Laura's shoulder. "We're indebted to you for the time you've spent giving Jonas the information he needed to understand your mother's people, Courtney. His concern for the Indians will be a key factor in his campaign to save the Everglades and put him over the top at election time. With Laura standing at his side...don't you think she'll make a terrific—and beautiful—first lady of the state of Florida?"

Cheers and toasts went up around the room. Fortunately Silas was beaming at the dynamic blond attorney and didn't notice Courtney's loss of color or her departure from the group. She ran to the bathroom where she could be sick. Where she could absorb the stunning blow in private.

Was it true? Courtney asked herself. Had Jonas's interest in her stemmed solely from a need to glean information about the tribe? Had Jonas always planned to marry Laura? Hadn't the precious time they'd spent together meant anything at all?

She couldn't take this in. Yet it had to be true for his own father to announce it in front of everyone. Was that the reason Jonas had been so anxious for the case to be settled? So he and Laura could make definite plans to marry?

In a state of shock, Courtney had finally crept back to the computer room for her handbag, wanting only to get out of there and never return. Of necessity, she had to pass Raynor Cox's office on her way to the exit. With his sly comments and innuendos, Cox was the one man in the firm who revolted her. As usual, Laura was with him. Courtney had never eavesdropped in her life, but his door was ajar and their conversation carried into the hallway.

"You have to give Jonas his due. Befriending our fetching little squaw has got the tribe eating out of his hand. Convincing them to sue the government over that old land treaty really paid off—with a big fat twenty-million-dollar settlement. His fee ought to take care of the campaign funding very nicely."

"That's what makes him governor material, Raynor."

"When are you two getting married?"

"We'll set the date after he gets back from Washington. Silas says Jonas will announce his candidacy at the same time."

"What about Courtney? He hasn't spent all his time pumping her for information, you know."

"She's never been a threat, Raynor. And never could be. Jonas says her grant will come through any day now and then she'll be off. Confidentially, he's concerned that she's taken his interest in her to mean more than it does. He's staying on in Washington a while longer, hoping she'll leave of her own accord. That way there won't be any messy ends to tie up."

"I'll be happy to take her off his hands if things get sticky," he murmured. The two of them chuckled.

Courtney couldn't bear to hear any more and fled the building. After scrambling into her truck, she drove for hours, with no destination in mind.

The earthshaking revelation that Jonas had never loved her and was using her to exploit the tribe for financial and political gain had caused the world to come crashing down around her. She hadn't been able to leave her job or Jonas's orbit fast enough.

Now an unexpected gust of wind rocked the airboat and broke in on Courtney's tortured thoughts. She glanced up at the black storm clouds. Normally, regardless of weather, she loved floating through this silent, prehistoric world with its labyrinths of marshland and hummocks, but the Glades in a downpour could be frightening to tourists. She realized she'd have to cut short the tour.

"Due to lack of time," she improvised, "we won't be docking at the island coming up on your left. But we'll pass close enough for you to observe an Indian family living much the same way as their tribesmen have lived since they escaped relocation to Oklahoma with their Seminole cousins in the 1800s."

"Correct me if I'm wrong, but I understood this tour included an hour's visit to the island," Jonas interjected.

"It's a rule of the Center that we always put the visitors' welfare first," she answered reasonably. "As you can see, it's going to rain. You'll all be more comfortable viewing the same artifacts and crafts in the museum." So saying, she headed the airboat back toward the main village.

On the return trip she entertained a fresh volley of questions from her passengers, including the people seated next to Jonas. For a brief moment, her gaze rested on him.

The familiar aquiline profile, the strong lines and angles of his arresting face, made Jonas physically perfect to Courtney. The potent male charisma and the strength of his personality had captivated her from the beginning—had blinded her to the self-serving man beneath.

The pain of his deceit was still so raw. Trying to shake it off she quickly channeled all her energy into piloting the airboat back to the dock.

But her panic grew as she calculated how she could escape him. Everything in her cried out to run, but under the circumstances, she couldn't do that. He was relentless when he pursued anything he wanted, and he wanted her, because she'd injured his pride, perhaps. Or because her flight had made her seem more desirable. Courtney knew he'd find her no matter where she went or how long it took him.

She efficiently docked the airboat, then unfastened the barrier. Fixing a smile in place, she turned to her tour group. "I want to thank you for being such an appreciative and understanding audience and I hope you'll come again soon. Don't forget the Indian Arts Festival held here in December and January. More than forty tribes gather to sing, dance and perform for the public.

"And please remember that you can help save the Glades by writing letters to the editor of any Florida newspaper, expressing your reverence for one of the world's greatest natural wonders. Thank you."

Courtney submitted to the usual round of picture-taking, then shook hands with all the passengers as they disembarked. Except Jonas. He leaned against the rail watching her and her heart plummeted to her feet.

"That was an impressive tour," he said when everyone else was out of earshot.

"You mean in spite of your efforts to humiliate me?" she asked heatedly. She wheeled around, starting to walk away, but Jonas intercepted her.

"Now that you're through here, it's time for our little talk. Suppose we have it over dinner."

Her jaw clenched. "Why is it that a man takes rejection so much harder than a woman? Or is it that the Payne pride can't take being turned down by a gullible little half-breed?"

Without waiting for a response, Courtney set off toward the parking lot at a brisk pace, dodging the tourists still milling about the grounds. She half expected Jonas to drag her back by the arm to prevent her from leaving, but to her surprise and relief, he let her go.

He was an intelligent, even brilliant attorney, she reminded herself. He could see that Courtney had learned the truth and that no purpose would be served by trying to explain his behavior.

That was exactly what she'd hoped would happen, but there was an ache in her chest as she gunned the gas pedal of the pickup and it screeched onto Highway 41, better known as the Tamiami Trail.

In her heart of hearts, she'd held on to the fragile hope that he'd come after her because he loved her. She'd even tried to believe he could offer a perfectly reasonable explanation for everything. What a fool she was....

Rain spattered the mosquito-encrusted windshield as she drove west, wiping the tears from her cheeks. Within minutes sheets of rain, aided by gusty winds, washed the surface of the glass completely clean.

Though the sun wouldn't set for several more hours, the heavy clouds blocked out the light. She could scarcely discern the marker indicating that the Trail had entered the Red Mangrove Reservation, home to a few hundred Miccosukee Indians.

She pulled up to the restaurant, turned off the engine and made a mad dash for the door to avoid a total drenching. No one was inside but Rosa.

"Hi," Courtney greeted the older woman with feigned enthusiasm. "How's business?"

"What do you think?" Rosa replied woodenly, but there was a decided gleam in her dark eyes. "You hungry?"

Courtney shook out her braid before finding a seat at one of the tables. "I should be," she answered cryptically, "but I think all I'll have is salad and coffee." She sat back in the chair and rubbed her temples where she could feel the beginning of a headache. Only a few minutes later, Rosa brought her meal to the the table.

The inevitable slice of fried pumpkin bread accompanied the salad. Rosa was rightfully proud of her bread and Courtney dutifully ate it between sips of hot, black coffee. But her thoughts were full of Jonas and she soon lost whatever appetite she'd had. The future loomed dark and lonely, without fulfillment.

Frank Bird, a man close to Courtney's age of twenty-six years, one of the tribe's mechanics, wandered in with his brother. He stared hard at Courtney, something he'd been doing a lot lately. It seemed he always managed to show up wherever she was on the reservation. She gave him a polite nod, noting from his drenched appearance that the rain hadn't diminished.

As she contemplated her salad without tasting or seeing it, she felt a prickling on the back of her neck—a kind of extrasensory perception—as she had the time a sea manatee followed the progress of her canoe through a remote waterway at Cape Sable. It had hovered just below the surface, but she'd known it was there.

Putting down her fork, she glanced over her shoulder to encounter Jonas's penetrating stare. She'd assumed he was back in Miami by now. *Why was he drawing this thing out to the bitter end?* To her recollection, cruelty wasn't a part of his nature. But then, she hadn't known the real Jonas at all.

She swallowed hard, acknowledging his dark attraction. Except for the modern-day shirt plastered to his broad shoulders and chest, he bore a surprising resemblance to Osceola, the handsome warrior of a bygone age, a man she'd fantasized about since childhood. It was a physical resemblance that had struck her, because of Jonas's build, his bronzed skin, his features, whenever she'd seen him striding into the office. Like Osceola, he possessed the authority and powerful presence of a natural leader. But Osceola had been a prince among his people, fierce, proud, courageous and loved. Not a traitor.

Cornered, Courtney had no choice but to face her enemy. Perhaps the best defense was to take the offensive. "Come and sit down, Jonas," she urged in a quiet voice. The Miccosukee were a shy people, but always polite to strangers. She could be no less under the circumstances, especially since creating a scene would only provide gossip, something she detested.

"I'm glad to see you decided to take me up on my dinner invitation," he muttered, pulling a chair from another table so he could join her. He raked a bronzed hand through his black hair, wet from the rain, and smiled at Rosa, who brought him coffee and took his dinner order.

The easy camaraderie between them told Courtney they were more than acquaintances; they'd become friends. Rosa laughed good-naturedly at his teasing before she returned to the counter. Jonas's ability to charm Rosa, of all people, made him seem particularly dangerous.

"You're covered in mud," Courtney observed.

He sat back in the chair and glanced down at his wet, stained shirt and shoes. "I came within inches of plowing into a truck much like yours that skidded off the highway in my direction. I stopped to help the driver push his truck back over the lip."

He'd had a close call, Courtney thought agitatedly. But she managed to keep her voice steady. "There's a utility sink off the kitchen where you can wash up. Rosa won't mind. While you're doing that, I'll see about getting you something dry to wear before you leave."

Angry lines marred his good looks. "Your concern is touching." He took long swallows of his coffee. "As it happens, I'm not going anywhere so don't think you can sneak out of here. You can't put me off forever, Courtney."

Before she could respond, Rosa served his dinner, bringing him an extra slice of pumpkin bread and a fresh mug of hot coffee. He ate and drank with obvious enjoyment, not seeming the least concerned that there was a lag in the conversation. Courtney wondered if his reticence signaled the proverbial calm before the storm. She felt her tension growing as she tried to understand his reasons for pursuing a dead relationship, an unwanted romance.

Perhaps he needed something more from her, if only her reassurance that he could still count on her to explain Miccosukee ways, maybe even interpret for him. In any event, she'd had all she could take and started to get up from the table. But his strong hand reached out and covered hers, preventing her from leaving.

"Don't try it, Courtney," he said in a dangerously soft voice. "I haven't even started with you yet."

His grip was firm and he meant what he said. Courtney sat down. She cast a quick glance around the now almost-full restaurant; customers, most of them known to her, had been coming in steadily. Because of her preoccupation with Jonas, she'd barely noticed until now. "Please let go of my hand," she whispered urgently. "People are staring."

His mouth thinned. "Let them. I want the truth from you. *Now!*"

"Jonas," she said in a frantic voice. "We can't talk here."

"For the conversation I have in mind, I agree," he said tightly. "We can have it in my car or at your place."

Her chest heaved as if she'd just run a great distance. Despite all her efforts to avoid a final confrontation, Jonas had succeeded in forcing everything into the open. "Your car would be too public." She didn't mention that his car would also be too confining...too *intimate*....

His keen eyes played over her face. "Then it's your place. Let's go." Reluctantly his hand released hers to pull a twenty-dollar bill from his wallet and deposit it on the table. He complimented Rosa on the dinner, and to Courtney's disgust the older woman actually preened.

Once more Courtney felt Frank's eyes on her as she and Jonas got up from the table. She began to think what Rosa had told her about Frank might be true, that he was interested in Courtney. She'd known him since childhood, but she simply couldn't respond to him or any other man, not after falling in love with Jonas.

For that reason, she didn't resist when Jonas put a possessive hand on her to escort her from the restaurant. It was better if Frank thought she was involved with someone else. Rosa had been badgering Courtney to be nice to Frank, not to hurt him.

But Courtney paid a price for the small deception. Her skin seemed to burn from the brief contact of Jonas's hand. It shamed her to realize that in spite of the heart-wrenching pain she'd suffered over this man's betrayal, her senses could still respond to his nearness.

The moment they stepped outside, she pulled away, anxious to put as much distance between them as possible.

CHAPTER TWO

NIGHT HAD FALLEN over the Everglades. Courtney welcomed the mistlike rain after the earlier torrential downpour. "My bungalow is down the road." She walked quickly, trying to avoid puddles as well as Jonas's assistance.

His black Ferrari looked incongruous next to the odd assortment of secondhand cars and trucks pulled up in front of Rosa's. Jonas paced his stride to stay even with her until they reached the cluster of cement-block houses.

"This is my unit," she said, opening her unlocked door and turning on the lights. He moved inside the small living room, dwarfing it.

She made a hurried survey of the pseudo-Danish-modern furniture, trying to picture it from his perspective. Considering his own beautiful estate on La Gorse Island, he probably found the sight before their eyes quite laughable. Particularly as some of the others used Courtney's place to store baskets and dolls until they could be sold at the Center.

"Where are all your things? he asked quietly. Throughout their relationship he'd been inside her small Miami apartment only a few times because they'd spent most of their time on the Payne yacht cruising the Florida Keys.

"Everything's in storage for a while. I rented this furnished." She spread her hands in front of her. "I know it's not...what you're used to, but it's home for the moment. Sit down and I'll get us a cold drink."

He stared at her moodily. "Since when have you ever felt the need to apologize to me for anything?"

"Was I doing that?" She spoke conversationally, adjusting the small table fan to blow directly onto the couch. "This place is like a furnace every night when I come in." She lifted the heavy braid and draped it over one shoulder. "All I have to offer is ginger ale," she added, going to the kitchen.

After a sustained pause he said, "Ginger ale will be fine."

When she returned, he reached for the drink she placed on the table, watching her movements over the rim of the glass as he took a long swallow. She hurried into the bedroom and pulled a man's tailored shirt from the hanger.

"Here. Change into this. It's one of several I inherited when my dad left for Zaire. The bathroom's down the hall."

His green eyes flickered as he got to his feet and began unbuttoning his shirt. "If it's all right with you, I'll change in here. You're an elusive creature, Courtney Blake, and to be perfectly honest, I'm not in the mood for another disappearing act tonight."

In seconds he'd peeled off the sodden, mud-stained garment and shrugged into the white cotton shirt, which emphasized his dark coloring and bronzed skin.

The sight of his powerful chest reminded her that it was weeks since she'd been in his arms, crushed against him until she couldn't tell his heartbeat from her own.

Something in her expression must have communicated itself to him because he whispered her name on a ragged breath. The raw blaze of desire in his eyes sent her flying toward the kitchen with his wet shirt in hand.

In an effort to rid herself of the longing his nearness evoked, she concentrated on filling the sink, then she put his shirt in to soak. Away from him she could see her path clearly, but this close, all she could think about was how he made her feel when he started making slow, exquisite love to her.

Maybe if she hadn't held back when he wanted to sleep with her, the fire inside her body wouldn't be burning so white-hot now. No other man had ever affected her as Jonas had. No one else had ever had the power to reduce her to this mindless desire to make her crave the fulfillment only he could offer. But the traditional values she'd learned from her mother prevented her from sleeping with a man unless he was her husband.

The man she eventually married would have to make her feel like this, but she doubted another such man existed. What really frightened her was that for the rest of her life she'd compare every man to Jonas.

She doubted she'd be able to give her heart so completely again.

"Courtney?" At the sound of her name she jerked around to see Jonas's lean frame propped against the doorjamb, his thumbs hooked inside his pockets. "Stop fiddling and come back to the living room. We have to talk. I think by now you must realize I'm not leaving."

Her hands shook as she squeezed the water out of his shirt and hung it over a chair to dry. "You never give up, do you, Jonas? I have to tell you it's not one of your more attractive qualities."

His eyes glittered with rage. "Being shrewish isn't one of yours. Forget the shirt. I have a housekeeper, remember?"

How could she not? Plus apartments and real estate in various parts of the world. He lacked for nothing. And she suspected that as far as the tribe went, he didn't need anything more from her.

So what did he want? Did he honestly think she'd continue to see him after his marriage, just because of the strong sexual attraction between them?

"More important, you're involved with Laura. *Remember?*" she exploded, clutching the chair back for support.

His dark brows furrowed. "We're both partners in the firm, if that's what you mean. Is she the one who called you a half-breed? Is that what this is all about?"

Courtney sucked in her breath. "I've been called many things in my life and I can handle that. What I can't tolerate is being taken for a fool. How long did you plan to keep me in the dark?''

''I don't know what in the hell you're talking about,'' he thundered.

''Stop lying to me, Jonas! I know all about you and Laura. The whole office knows!'' Her hands balled into fists.

''Knows what?'' he demanded. ''Don't stop now. Enlighten me.''

''How can you pretend not to know what I'm talking about when your father's announced your wedding plans to the entire staff!''

In the dimly lit kitchen, Jonas's face looked ashen. ''When did all this take place?''

She lifted her chin proudly. ''On the night your case was settled. Silas called everyone in for a celebration toast in honor of your winning that twenty-million-dollar suit. I overheard Laura tell Raynor you'd be making marriage arrangements as soon as you returned from Washington.''

There was an interminable silence. ''And you believed *them* after everything we've meant to each other?'' His voice was tightly controlled, but a cord stood out in his neck, revealing his anger.

Courtney's eyes opened wide. ''Are you asking me to believe your father and Laura would lie to a roomful of people? Their co-workers, no less?''

''I'm not asking you to believe it. I'm telling you straight out that anything you heard the other night was pure fabrication.''

She shook her head in disbelief. "I knew there was a rift between you and your father, but I had no idea it was so serious."

"Why are you defending him, Courtney? Where's the warm, loving woman I held in my arms two weeks ago? I could have sworn that woman believed in me."

His words, spoken with such fervor, confused Courtney and brought back a flood of memories. She almost ran into the living room to put distance between them.

Jonas appeared in the doorway seconds later, his face grim and uncompromising. The drone of the fan seemed to underline the tension in the air. "So we've both been living in a fairy tale." He sounded strangely remote.

"Why did you pretend to be in love with *me?*" she cried out in pain. "Did you derive some kind of sick pleasure from humiliating me? I would have given you what you were after. All you had to do was ask."

His mouth had thinned into a white line of anger.

"If I wasn't in love with you, then would you mind telling me what you think I wanted from you?"

"You wanted clout with the tribe, so you condescended to date me, giving you access to all the inside information you needed about Miccosukee life. And you hoped that as my supposed fiancé, you'd have an unprecedented entrée with the tribal elders, which would give you credibility in their eyes."

There was a sharp intake in breath. "That's a fascinating supposition. But the fact of the matter is, Chief Bob Willie doesn't approve of your life-style,

Courtney. You remind him of one of his sons, who left the reservation a few years back to make it in the white world. The chief's a traditionalist. If anything, being involved with you has caused me to lose face with him.''

Courtney's cheeks went several shades of red before losing color completely. The astuteness of his remark left her breathless. Courtney was well aware of the chief's feelings; they weren't that different from Rosa's. What astounded her was Jonas's being privy to that kind of information. It cut the ground from under her.

He took a step closer. ''Have I ever once in our relationship asked you to use your influence with the chief?''

Courtney couldn't sustain his glance. ''No. Obviously you exert a powerful influence in your own right,'' she said with vicious sarcasm, ''and you've appealed to his sense of pride. I give you full credit for manipulating him so subtly and expertly, that he had no idea what you were after.''

An ominous quiet followed her statement. ''And what was that?''

''You know very well we're talking about money. A lot of money.''

''I'm a wealthy man, Courtney. But let's presume for the moment that I'm greedy for more. Explain to me how manipulating the chief would benefit me, when he's the tribal head of one of the poorer Indian nations in North America.''

"Do you deny you researched that old treaty and discovered it had enough flaws to be challenged in a court of law?"

"You already know the answer to that because I told you about it."

"But the tribal elders didn't understand the legal ramifications until you explained them."

"That's right."

"So you convinced Bob Willie and the others to sue the government, knowing there'd be a lucrative settlement if you won the case."

"That's right. They'd get back their original parcel of land and a cash settlement on the interest owing them."

She glared at Jonas. "And of course you're not keeping a dime of it."

A dark brow quirked. "I didn't say that. As a matter of fact, I've retained a considerable amount for a ... project I'm working on."

A tight band around her chest constricted Courtney's breathing. "And we both know what that is. So you're no different from other lawyers in the past who've taken advantage of the Indian and pocketed the majority of the proceeds with no thought for the tribe's needs."

"Be very careful of what you're saying, Courtney. Contrary to some people's belief, your Indian blood doesn't give you psychic knowledge of my motives." His tone was threatening. And worse, contemptuous.

Courtney backed up against a chair in alarm. "Jonas—" She put a hand to her throat. "I'd like you to go now."

"Dear Lord," he muttered, "to think I actually believed we could've had a future together."

Her body went cold from the hostility in his voice. "I—I did everything in my power to prevent this from happening tonight, but you—"

"Don't you dare presume one more thing where I'm concerned." He moved toward her and she shrank from the menace in his expression. "You have it all figured out, don't you?" His eyes were the green of an angry ocean.

She took an involuntary step back but his hand shot out and seized her wrist, holding her fast. "For the sake of curiosity," he hissed, "tell me about this nefarious project I'm working on."

A tremor passed through Courtney's body. "Don't do this, Jonas." But he wasn't listening.

"Tell me!" His grip tightened.

"The funding for your campaign."

His mouth twisted nastily. "Whatever my father told you, I'm not running for political office, Courtney. I considered it once, but that was a long time ago. Things have changed quite drastically since the days when my father and I saw eye to eye on what was best for me."

Her head reeled and if he hadn't been holding her, she would have fallen to the floor.

His eyes flickered. "I don't understand the man's influence on you! It's so strong you didn't have the decency or the courage—or the respect for me—to tell me what went on at the office that hurt you so badly. Our whole relationship was in the balance. And you ran away."

His tight grasp on her arm told her his control was barely in check. "You knew damn well what happened to us comes once in a lifetime, if at all. You owed it to me, to yourself, to our happiness, to call me. I could have explained. We could have talked things out."

Perhaps it was her imagination, but she thought she saw a flash of pain in the dark recesses of his eyes. Unexpectedly, he let go of her arm.

"I'd give anything to believe you," she whispered brokenheartedly.

He flashed her a look she couldn't decipher. "You're not the woman for me, after all. You may be one of the most beautiful creatures God ever put on this earth, but you're pure ice on the inside—brittle, unbending, incapable of faith. And so help me, frozen to the very core. I don't know why I ever thought there was a way to melt you."

He crossed the room in a few swift strides and disappeared out the front door before she could call him back.

Hours later she was still crying scalding tears into her pillow. The scene in the living room had accomplished what all the evasion tactics in the world hadn't been able to do. Jonas had gone for good.

The pain was so excruciating, she wondered if she might actually die of it.

Sleep must have come to her at some point during the night because she began dreaming of Jonas. But it was a Jonas wearing Osceola's leggings, turban and jacket with the distinctive shoulder pouches labeling him the hero of his people. He smiled for everyone but her. Courtney woke up to a wet pillow, profoundly disturbed that, awake or asleep, Jonas haunted her.

Wishing her mother were still alive to comfort her, she got up from the bed and walked slowly to the dresser where she kept pictures of her parents, as well as a small wooden carving of Osceola that her mother had treasured. A wistful expression broke out on Courtney's tearstained face as she thought about her mother, a woman torn between two cultures.

Traditionally, the Miccosukee didn't talk of physical attraction. If the woman was a good cook, the man a good hunter, those were the qualities that made a good wife or husband. Yet Courtney's mother had loved Thomas Blake for many other reasons, other qualities, and had ultimately married him. Courtney's gaze went to his picture for a moment. He was a loving father, a hardworking engineer. He was also white, with sensitive blue eyes and auburn hair like Courtney's.

She'd always thought it was his all-American looks and his expansive, open personality that had drawn her mother. On a deep sigh Courtney turned away. Her parents had been complete opposites—contrasting personalities in every sense—and that had formed the basis of their attraction. *Like mother, like daughter?* But with Jonas she'd always shared so much, and their differences had enhanced their love, not imperiled it . . . Or so she'd believed. . . .

She didn't know why Jonas had felt it necessary to lie to her, didn't understand the animosity he harbored toward his father. But a parent as devoted as Silas wouldn't have behaved the way he had at the office unless he was telling the truth. From the first day on the job, Courtney had been aware of Silas's affection for his only son. Jonas was his golden boy.

Silas reminded Courtney a little of her own father. Thomas Blake had doted on his daughter, probably because she, too, was an only child. She could do no wrong in his eyes. He'd always backed her in any project, assuring her no dream was impossible to attain if it was what she wanted.

She could sense Silas was the same kind of father, a man who wanted nothing but the best for his son. Courtney couldn't help admiring Silas for his fierce pride in Jonas's success. Though it pained her to admit it, she could understand why he wanted Laura for a daughter-in-law.

Laura was a successful, ambitious woman, groomed for public life. She'd complement Jonas in a way Courtney never could, and be the perfect mate for a man whose future would keep him in the limelight.

Courtney had had this point reaffirmed even more emphatically the morning after the champagne celebration, when she went into Silas's office to tell him she was quitting. She could still recall Silas's phone conversation with one of his friends, Mark Tolman, an important Realtor.

"That's right, Mark" he was saying, "Jonas had to pay his dues for a while and sink his teeth into a few projects, which were, uh, somewhat delicate in nature. But now that one of his big cases is over, he and Laura are making plans. Everything's finally in place for him to put in his bid with the party."

While he talked, he flashed Courtney a broad, white smile reminiscent of Jonas's and signaled that he was almost through, for her to wait.

"That's where you come in, Mark," he finished, "but I'll tell you all about it tonight at the house when you come for dinner. Blanche says we'll be serving cocktails at seven."

His conversation had sounded the death knell in her heart all over again, forcing her to suffer in silence until she could leave the law firm permanently.

Now thankful that morning had finally come, Courtney showered and dressed in clean denims and a blouse. After hanging Jonas's shirt in the closet so she wouldn't constantly be reminded of him, she left the house to get the canoe an uncle had carved for her years earlier. It was in the storage shed behind Rosa's place.

Courtney used the canoe when she went to visit her grandmother, who lived in the Glades. However, since the death of her mother three years earlier, Courtney hadn't been to see her family as often as she would have liked. Her university studies had kept her too busy to take much time off.

In fact, her project in Oklahoma would take a year and a half to complete. The Muskogee language spoken by the Seminole Indians in Oklahoma was related to the language of the Miccosukee. Courtney planned to do a comparative study of the two languages as part of her post-doctoral program.

When that was completed, her mentor, Dr. Egli, had informed her she'd be asked to join the anthropology department on a full-time teaching basis. But Courtney couldn't possibly leave for Oklahoma without visiting her relatives first. Who knew when she'd have the opportunity to spend much time with them again in the near future?

The thought of being in their undemanding company went a long way to ease the ache in her heart. She needed to be with her grandmother because it brought her a little closer to her own mother.

Not only that, the aging matriarch, estimated to be in her late eighties, was a walking encyclopedia of information. With her rested the memories of a little-known world that was fast disappearing. Courtney wanted to record her stories, for the tribe and for herself.

Right now she was anxious to be off. The physical exertion of the trip alone would help allay the pain of her betrayal by Jonas. And once she arrived, she'd have enough to do, at least during the day—joining in the work, playing with the children, talking with her grandmother—to keep thoughts of Jonas from disturbing her. It was the nights she had to worry about.

She concealed her puffy eyes behind sunglasses and hoped no one was outside the restaurant to notice her extreme pallor. The thought of food nauseated her, so she didn't intend to stop for breakfast. But to her dismay, she saw Chief Bob Willie waiting for her beside her truck, still parked in front of Rosa's.

It wasn't until she walked around to the driver's side that she caught sight of Jonas. He was lounging against the door of a mud-spattered truck, bearing the GSA insignia from the Bureau of Indian Affairs, parked next to her pickup. *What was going on?*

She took off her glasses and stared helplessly at the two men. Her gaze focused on Jonas, who was informally dressed in khakis and safari shirt. He looked vital and aggressively masculine, but when she studied his face, it wore the remote expression of a stranger.

She quickly darted a glance at Bob Willie for an explanation. He nodded and said hello.

"Bob," she replied.

"You want to come into the city with us? Since you used to work for Jonas, you could help translate while he talks to Tommie. He needs help."

She took a deep breath, avoiding Jonas's pitiless stare. Tommie was Bob's oldest son, and she'd heard he'd got into some trouble. "Is he in Miami?"

"That's right, and Jonas has been doing some investigating for us."

Courtney shook her head as if to clear it. "I don't understand. This is a civil problem, not a land matter."

Bob's stoical expression gave nothing away. "Maybe Rosa was wrong. Maybe she saw another man go into your house last night. That must be the explanation. Otherwise you'd know Jonas Payne is the new superintendent for Red Mangrove Reservation."

CHAPTER THREE

"WHAT?" SHE THOUGHT she couldn't have heard Bob correctly and switched her gaze to Jonas.

"It doesn't surprise me you find the idea ludicrous," he said in an aloof tone, obviously enjoying her discomfiture.

She smoothed a few tendrils of dark chestnut hair from her forehead. "I don't understand. How could you possibly become a superintendent?" For a moment, Bob was forgotten.

"How does anyone?" he asked with a hint of irony.

"It's a job given to Native American Indians who've spent years working up through the ranks!"

"Not always," he corrected her. "In my case, the tribal council voted for me, and on that basis I was politically appointed. It happens on occasion—even to a white man."

Courtney looked at Bob for verification. The chief gave her one of his rare smiles. "That's right. More than a year ago we approached him. Mr. Payne's done excellent work for us in land negotiations, and the tribe was unanimous in wanting him to oversee reservation business. He's had a lot to study and learn but now it's official."

No wonder he'd monopolized every moment of Courtney's free time! She could hardly breathe. "When did this happen?"

Jonas studied her tightened features for a long moment. "I received the appointment while I was in Washington."

Courtney still reeled from the impact of Bob Willie's disclosure. The political appointment of a white man was so rare an occurrence, she couldn't remember a single case unless she went back to the turn of the century, when there was one rather remarkable white "agent," as they were called then.

A superintendent's job was a lifetime career commitment, coordinating and administering federal policies within the framework of the reservation.

The Payne family had friends in high places, but not even they could arrange for this appointment unless the tribe had been one hundred percent behind Jonas. She couldn't fathom it!

Were they all blind to Jonas's exploitation tactics? He had no intention of spending the rest of his life on Red Mangrove! This was nothing more than a clever career move. A public relations maneuver, part of his strategy to ensure the vote. And how was he going to handle his heavy caseload at the firm? Who had the expertise and brilliance to cover for him when he wasn't in the office?

"Why didn't you tell me this last night?"

He straightened to his full, imposing height. "The reason is no longer relevant."

She couldn't have been more shocked if he'd slapped her. Had he *ever* intended to tell her? He'd carefully kept his secret during the months they'd spent together, saying nothing about his plans or ambitions. Jonas was the consummate actor! It appeared running for governorship was just a matter of time, now. His protestations of the night before—*I'm not running for political office, Courtney*—seemed even more laughable and insincere in the light of this appointment. Becoming a superintendent had to be one of those "delicate" projects Silas had mentioned. Jonas was on his way to the top. Never mind that he had no real interest in Indian affairs beyond the political one.

Courtney was beginning to see that going to court over an ancient treaty was only part of a much bigger plan. She should have known. Jonas was carving out his destiny.

She tossed her glossy braid over her shoulder. "A superintendent's supposed to be on call day and night for reservation business. How do you think you'll manage that and stay on top of things at the firm?"

"If you hadn't quit your job, you'd know the answer to that question," he said scornfully. "The fact is, I've left the firm."

"For how long?" She tried to keep her voice steady.

"For good."

The revelations coming one on top of the other staggered her. "But all your clients—"

"They'll be turned over to capable hands. Unlike you, I won't run off and leave everything in a muddle before closing the door forever."

His reminder of her hasty departure from the office didn't go unnoticed. "Don't tell me you're going to live on the reservation!" The thought had just occurred to her.

"I'd like to be able to say yes, simply to enjoy the look on your face. But as it happens, I plan to live at home and enjoy all my worldly goods. When an emergency arises, I can commute by helicopter. Now, do you have any other questions you want to ask, or shall we concentrate on Tommie's problems?"

Jonas enjoyed putting her in the wrong, especially in front of Bob, who'd never approved of her living in the city. Still, she would never be intentionally rude to the chief; she realized that, in his way, he tried to look out for her. "Bob?" She turned to face him. "Why do you think you need me?"

"Because Tommie trusts you, and Jonas feels a bilingual translator will ensure that everything is understood correctly."

It was on the tip of her tongue to tell Bob she was an anthropologist, not a translator, but of course she couldn't do that. She liked the chief, and liked his son. They were family friends. Jonas was another matter, and she returned her attention to him. "Doesn't the Bureau provide translators when necessary?"

"Of course they do. You know that. But I've had some meetings with Tommie and he'd like you there because he considers you a friend, as well as someone who's comfortable in both worlds.'' He regarded her steadily until the warmth crept up her neck. In any encounter, Jonas always managed to come out ahead.

"I can't see that my translating services are needed. Tommie can speak English.'' Still, she knew that Tommie was shy and awkward around strangers, apt to respond in monosyllables.

There was an uncomfortable silence before Jonas said, ''Poor communication is the reason there's always been distrust between the Bureau and the tribe. If you don't want to help, just say so.''

Jonas's reference to poor communications was not only accurate but shrewd. It put her in the position of being petty if she wasn't amenable to helping. ''What exactly did Tommie do?''

"He's been charged with killing a panther within the Park boundaries.''

Her head shot up. ''Tommie wouldn't do that!'' she said. Of all the chief's sons, Tommie was the gentlest, the kindest, the one who most loved nature and never ventured far from the reservation. He, more than anyone, knew the panther was an endangered species; he also knew perfectly well that anyone killing a panther broke the law and suffered severe penalties.

"Well, you've told me one thing I wanted to know anyway,'' he said dryly, glancing at his watch. ''We have to get going if we're to do anything about his situation today. Are you coming or not?''

Bob suddenly spoke in Miccosukee. ''Rosa was right, after all. You and Jonas strike sparks. You're like your mother.''

It might have been a harmless observation, but as far as Courtney was concerned, Bob had gone too far. "Do you want my help with Tommie?" she answered in the same tongue.

"Sure."

"Then I would appreciate it if we talked about Tommie."

"That's okay with me," he said reverting to English. "Let's go."

Within minutes they were off in Jonas's truck, traveling over roads surrounded by swampland, prairie, and hummocks covered with palmetto and cabbage palm. Courtney still felt the touch of Jonas's hand where it had brushed accidentally against her thigh as she climbed into the backseat. It made her far too aware of him.

She looked out the window at the passing landscape but nothing made an impression because she was completely preoccupied with Jonas's unexpected reappearance in her life. His impressive new title placed him squarely in her orbit, a possibility she wouldn't have imagined in her wildest dreams.

Yesterday she'd believed he was gone from her life forever. Now, incredibly, she was in his truck, driving into Miami on official business with him. Yet they'd never been farther apart.

Jonas didn't look as if last night's devastating scene had affected him in the slightest. Yet he had only to glance at her to know how deeply it had affected her.

She'd have to make an effort to pull herself together for Tommie's sake, but it was almost impossible when she was hurting so terribly.

Jonas's charm reached out to everyone around him. Rosa, Bob Willie—no one was immune. When she could get the chief alone, she planned to warn him that Jonas's great show of interest and sensitivity was just a pretense, part of his effort to climb the political ladder. The trouble was, would Bob believe her? Already the two of them displayed a camaraderie rarely seen with the older man.

A half hour later the towers of Miami came into view, the sun glinting from their smoked glass and steel. There was no sign of rain this morning. Courtney gazed out at the endless string of fast-food establishments lining the highway. It never ceased to amaze her that the teeming metropolis of Miami thrived virtually next door to the remote and strangely beautiful Everglades.

Jonas drove to the Municipal Complex, and it wasn't long before they'd arrived at the jail to talk to Tommie. Jonas interviewed the nineteen-year-old for an hour, frequently calling on Courtney for clarification. Bob listened quietly and occasionally made a comment or nodded his head. Then Jonas excused himself. He disappeared for a while and when he returned, Tommie had been released on bail. The four of them stopped for barbecued chicken before returning to the reservation.

Jonas drove to Rosa's and walked Bob and his son to their pickup truck. He waved off their thanks, reminding them that Tommie mustn't hunt until the case was closed.

Climbing out of the truck, Courtney smiled her acknowledgment as the two men thanked her and Jonas again. When they'd left, Jonas turned to look at her, and she met his level gaze.

"You used your own money to get him released. Why?"

"Because I know he didn't kill that panther, and soon I'll have the name of the guilty party."

Her finely arched brows drew together. "But Tommie didn't give you any hard evidence."

"That's true," he murmured, "but I've learned a lot from you over the past couple of months and certain things simply didn't add up."

"What things?"

Jonas leaned against the truck with his arms folded. "One night you talked at length about the Miccosukee, that they only hunt what they need for food or survival. The panther provides neither in Tommie's case. Being Bob Willie's son, he knows the law and wouldn't dare break it or he'd have his father to deal with, not just the courts."

Despite everything, Courtney felt a grudging respect for Jonas perceptiveness.

"Then you think it was that gang of rowdy whites from Naples, the ones Tommie identified?"

"I know it was. I had an autopsy performed on that panther. It died of head injuries from the wheel of the supercharged Chev Tommie saw on State Road 9336. The bullet wound in the panther's leg was superficial and couldn't have been made by the bullets from Tommie's gun.

"I've traced the car to Naples and should have a name shortly. It was Tommie's misfortune to be in the area when the rangers discovered the panther."

"What about his hunting in the Park?"

"The judge let it go. Indian rights predate the law. The Glades have been their hunting grounds for centuries, so no court is going to challenge Tommie's right to hunt in an area that has been his backyard since birth. But I've warned him to stay permanently away from the tourist areas."

Courtney nodded in agreement. What he'd done for Tommie was going to be big news and entrench him more firmly in the tribe's affection. But in all honesty, Courtney had to admit it was a kind thing for Jonas to do. "I'm sure Tommie's thankful. Being behind bars would be the worst form of torture for him. He's getting married soon. Now he can go ahead with his plans."

"Thank you for helping. He was more free with his answers and supplied some important details I needed to present to the judge. Your presence made a real difference."

Courtney looked away, unaccountably troubled by his sincerity. It reminded her of the Jonas she'd fallen in love with, before he destroyed her dreams.

"There'll be another hearing once I've gathered all the evidence. Tommie will want you there."

She hugged her arms to her waist. "When do you think that will be?"

"Some time next week if I can arrange it. Why? Planning to disappear again?" he mocked. "Don't do it on my account, Courtney. It would be wasted energy."

She felt her breathing constrict. "I asked because I won't be here next week. I'm going to my grandmother's on Saturday morning."

His mouth hardened. "For how long?"

"A month."

"How far is the settlement from here?"

"If it isn't raining, I can paddle my canoe there in a day. But if we have any more downpours, it'll probably take two days."

"Where does she live, *exactly?*"

"In the Red Mangrove Preserve near the Okaloacoochee Slough. The hummock has enough soil for the family to raise crops. It's noted for the profusion of lavender flowers that grow there. But she doesn't have a post office box."

He ran his hand through his black hair, disheveling it. "Are you making the trip alone?" he asked, choosing to ignore her sarcasm.

"Yes," she said. She'd never touched on these personal details in their earlier conversations. "My mother sent me on my first trip there alone when I was sixteen. I've been doing it ever since. My mother was living in one of the reservation houses then, which is where I used to visit her. But it was expected that I spend some time at my grandmother's, too."

"Over the river and through the woods," he muttered. "How did your father feel about your going alone?"

Courtney stirred restlessly at his persistence. "He didn't know because I didn't tell him. As you know, my parents separated after I was born. When I was old enough to go to school, I lived with him nine months of the year and spent the summers with my mother. He loved her enough not to ask too many questions or make impossible demands. My mother was very independent."

"Did she return his love?"

"Yes. So much so that she gave me to him." Her eyes misted. "She didn't want me to experience the trauma of trying to fit in his world and then being rejected by her own."

"Rejected?" One dark brow arched in disbelief.

"My father wasn't allowed to live with Mother on the reservation, so they were married in his church in Fort Lauderdale. They made a home there but my mother couldn't adjust. Even though she graduated from high school and went to junior college before she met Father, she was too set in her ways.

"I think she felt strange in Father's world. It just didn't work out. But when she first returned to the reservation she was snubbed. So I was born at my grandmother's hut. Father visited us often, and when I reached kindergarten age, he took me with him. Later on, Mother lived next door to Rosa."

"And were you snubbed?"

"Not exactly. I'm more of a curiosity than anything."

A long silence ensued. "I thought you were planning to visit your father soon."

Jonas never forgot anything. "I am, after I've finished up here."

"Then why the trip to your grandmother's?"

Because I need the comfort that only my family can give me right now, and it's all because of you. "I've missed the family. I'm especially anxious to see my grandmother again. She's had an interesting life. And also, I'd like to get her stories on tape before she passes on."

Jonas looked pensive. "In that case I won't schedule another hearing until your return. Have a safe trip." With a curt nod of his dark head, he got back into the truck and drove off.

"I will," she whispered to the empty air, feeling an ache too deep for tears. Something was very wrong. She'd made the break with Jonas and he wanted nothing more to do with her, so why did a life that didn't include him sound utterly insupportable—despite everything she knew?

Probably because for the past two months they'd been inseparable. There had been quiet times of sharing and loving, but they'd played, too. Jonas had a passion for skin-diving and had infected her with his love of the sport. How could all their closeness have been an act on his part? She could have sworn he loved her. During their months together Laura might never have existed. Or so Courtney had thought.

Angry with herself for her ambivalence, she marched behind Rosa's place and walked right through a mud puddle on the way to the shed. She had the awful premonition that nothing was ever going to be the same again, certainly not while Jonas was superintendent of Red Mangrove.

If he'd been approached as long as a year ago about the position, why hadn't he ever mentioned it to Courtney? Had the chief told him not to say anything until it was official? Or had Jonas decided it wasn't worth discussing because he planned to cut Courtney out of his life once she'd served her purpose? That explanation made the most sense.

For the next few days Courtney spent her time recording interviews with residents of the reservation during the day, and putting the conversations on disk at her personal computer. The computer filed the words and built a vocabulary list accordingly. Every sound had to be identified and given a symbol. It was a tedious, painstaking process, but a necessary one if she intended to develop a written language.

A handful of people, mostly nineteenth-century missionaries, had attempted something similar. But Courtney's contribution, which was part of her dissertation, would be by far the most complete, the most sophisticated and the most up-to-date. And she was aided by the fact that her formative years had been spent speaking Miccosukee.

On Friday afternoon, Courtney tidied the house and made final preparations for her journey. Her canoe had been placed at the put-in point on the water route leading north. Judging by all the paraphernalia she had to take in the way of recorders, batteries and tapes, not to mention her stores and camping equipment, the canoe would ride low in the water. Normally she wouldn't be concerned, but the weather bureau forecast a tropical storm in the next few days that could make boat travel precarious.

Under the circumstances, she went to bed before nine so she could get an early start the next morning. If she could reach the halfway point before the wind made things unmanageable, she'd be all right. Unfortunately she had trouble getting to sleep and awakened tired and out of sorts. It galled her to admit that Jonas was the cause of her insomnia.

She'd seen nothing of him since the day they'd driven into Miami. She assumed he was putting in long hours at the firm to finish up business, and could imagine that the rest of his time was taken up with Laura. Just the thought of Laura in his arms, Laura being kissed by him, sent Courtney from her bed to the shower to get ready for her trip.

A low ceiling of clouds didn't augur well for the journey as she paddled away from shore in the predawn. Even a water moccasin coiled like a fire hose around a melaleuca tree, waiting for its unsuspecting prey, seemed less alert than it should have been. In the distance, one lone kite hovered over the surface of the water, ready to pluck out an apple snail for breakfast.

She missed the noisy accompaniment of birdsong as she maneuvered the canoe silently and expertly over a carpet of swamp lilies toward an open waterway. The strong pull of the current told her the winds were building over the Ten Thousand Islands.

She paddled faster and harder through the open water and stopped at noon to eat a sandwich near the great white herons' rookery, the first of the landmarks by which she navigated through the Everglades. This was her favorite hummock, an island of earth and trees in the saw grass. It was a place of enchantment that offered protection from the wind, but she didn't have time to rest in the deserted chickee—a roofed hut with no sides—one of many dotting the Glades.

She paddled on, past a strangler fig that camouflaged a tree in its deadly embrace. At this time next year the host tree would be gone. Where would *she* be? she wondered.

Intense loneliness filled her as she grieved for the loss of Jonas. She loved him, she admitted bleakly, loved him desperately in spite of everything and couldn't get him out of her mind.

Distressed that she could have been so wrong about him, that he wasn't the person she'd thought he was, she started to increase her speed. But at that moment she knew she wasn't alone. The odd prickling on the back of her neck warned her of another presence.

She broke rhythm to glance over her shoulder. Nothing appeared to disturb the steamy silence. In the nine years she'd been coming here alone, she'd never met another canoeist. The area was too remote and inhospitable. It had to be a Miccosukee out hunting.

Taking a deep breath, she determined to make up time and struck out hard and fast. She had to get across the broad lagoon by early evening in order to set up camp on the next hummock. It would be the only dry mound within miles at this season.

When she was midway across the open body of water, the waves turned into whitecaps. Courtney's speed was cut to a mere crawl, and she feared her canoe would be swamped. Calling on inner strength and all the navigational skills at her command she slowly made headway, but it was an agonizing process of gain and loss.

Deep in concentration, she let out a cry of surprise when her paddle dug into the hard back of a large alligator. It had evidently been swimming parallel to her canoe only a few inches below the boiling water.

Perspiration broke out on her body as she used the paddle to deflect the smack of its tail against the canoe. A big wave surged over the bow at exactly the same moment, completely soaking her. At this rate her canoe would be swamped, and all her precious recording equipment ruined or lost.

For the first time in her life she knew real fear. Several more waves like that and she'd have no protection from the alligator, which had come close enough to nudge the canoe off course.

In a desperate, futile attempt to put even a few feet between herself and the alligator, she tried maneuvering the canoe in a semicircle. It was then she saw a kayaker paddling toward her with astonishing speed. She had only a brief glimpse of a man with dark hair before he drew alongside the alligator, daringly skimming by its side to draw its attention. *Jonas! She couldn't believe it!*

CHAPTER FOUR

"COURTNEY?" HE SHOUTED. "Keep on going while I lead him away. I'll meet you on the other side." With the skill resulting from years of practice, Jonas paddled through the waves and the alligator followed, giving Courtney the respite she needed to rid the canoe of excess water and veer toward the small inlet that led to an ancient Calusa mound, part of the remains of an Indian settlement dating back to the 1500s.

It was a battle against the elements as she approached the shore. Jonas drew up fifteen minutes later in his kayak, unsnapped the skirt and leaped out to help her pull the canoe farther up on the saw grass outcrop.

The wind made it next to impossible to maneuver. She'd reached the end of her strength. When Jonas saw the amount of water still in the bottom of the canoe he swore softly, and his eyes found hers in a searching glance. "Are you all right?"

"Yes," she whispered shakily and nodded her head, too full of gratitude to express it. Thrilled to see him, she wondered where he'd come from and why, but offered up a prayer of thanksgiving nonetheless.

"If you'll make camp for us, I'll start unloading the canoe. Let's hope your equipment isn't ruined."

She moistened her dry lips and flicked her gaze to the weather-worn chickee standing a few yards away on higher ground. "We can spread the bags, along with everything else, on the floor of the hut. It's going to rain in a minute."

Jonas scanned the dark sky. "I'll hurry." While Courtney was changing into dry clothes, he began making trips to the chickee with her gear. Once he'd finished, he brought his own things, from the kayak.

Courtney helped him overturn the canoe to dump the water out. "Let's carry this up to the chickee and turn it on its side to use for a windbreak," Jonas suggested.

The months she'd spent with him had revealed his ability to handle himself in the outdoors, and that expertise was never more in evidence than now. Jonas's intervention gave Courtney, who'd learned to do so many things alone, the rare sensation of being protected and cared for. It sent a warmth through her body and made her feel an unexpected closeness to him in spite of everything.

"That's a Miccosukee trick, in case you didn't know. I'm beginning to think you have some Indian blood in you," she teased, in an attempt to disguise her feelings, which were threatening to surface.

He lifted his end of the canoe and shot her a wicked glance. "I hate to disappoint you, but this is an old pirate trick. According to family stories, I'm descended from a black-haired buccaneer who terrorized every settlement in the Caribbean."

"I stand corrected," she quipped, wondering if he'd made that up. In all of Silas Payne's boasting, there had never been mention of that particular story before. But it would certainly account for Jonas's remarkable coloring, which he'd obviously inherited from his mother, a gentle woman Courtney had met on several occasions and liked very much.

Courtney lifted her end of the canoe and together they started walking. The physical demands of making camp kept her from dwelling too deeply on the night ahead of them and Jonas's reasons for following her in the first place. If he hadn't appeared when he had...

"Don't think about it," he murmured in a husky voice as they set the canoe in place against the wind. "It's over now."

She nodded without saying anything and avoided his eyes, amazed he could read her thoughts. "I brought a tarp."

"So did I. If you'll fix the coffee, I'll put up a couple of makeshift walls."

Out of the corner of her eye she watched Jonas shake out the tarps and survey the chickee intently. "All the comforts of home," he drawled, aware of her furtive glance. "What's this made of?" he asked, ever curious, as he attached ropes to the ridgepole.

"The palmetto tree."

"I think the floor might just be big enough to accommodate us and our gear." With a few more adjustments, Jonas had fashioned them a fairly secure shelter. As he finished tying down the bottom of the tarp the rain started.

"I'd say our timing couldn't have been more perfect." He got up from his crouched position and looked over at her as she primed the Coleman stove. One corner of his mouth curved enticingly. "I don't believe my eyes. I thought, of course, I'd learn how to light a fire Miccosukee style. I think I'm disappointed."

Courtney chuckled. "I try to incorporate the best of both worlds." In a matter of minutes she had coffee and beef stew ready. Jonas dipped into his pack and brought out a loaf of French bread and cheese. By tacit agreement they sat next to each other on a blanket Jonas had placed on the split-log flooring. Above their heads a lighted lantern hung from the poles.

The rain came down as if the heavens were emptying, sealing the two of them off from the rest of the world. Evening had come to the Everglades, but the storm created the illusion of darkest night. The rain cooled the air somewhat, though high humidity still made Courtney uncomfortably warm and sticky.

Jonas's shirt was damp in patches and tendrils of his black hair curled on the back of his neck. In such close quarters she could smell the male tang of his body mixed with the soap he always used. Right now she was aware of everything about him, especially his lithe, hard body, which moved with such controlled, masculine grace.

She was reminded of other moments when they'd lazed about on the yacht after snorkeling over the Coral Reef, but at times like those, someone was always around—a friend or a member of the crew, who could walk in on them. And at his house Courtney could never forget the presence of his housekeeper and gardener.

But here in the depths of the Glades they were totally alone, and the mere thought sent a delicious shiver through her trembling body.

"Jonas." She swallowed hard. "I would have lost all my equipment today if it hadn't been for you."

He put down his coffee mug. "That mightn't have been all you lost," he said thickly. "I know seasoned wilderness fanatics who wouldn't dare penetrate the Glades alone, and certainly not without a weapon handy."

"Is that why you came? To protect me?" she asked with her heart in her throat. There was a protracted silence.

"Someone should have done it long before now."

In the tension-filled moment, she poured herself another cup of coffee. "What's the *real* reason? After the other night—"

"I'm in charge of this territory now," he broke in, "and everything that happens falls under my jurisdiction. Even Indian maidens in distress."

She had the feeling he wasn't telling the truth. "You followed me all the way from Red Mangrove."

Jonas broke off another hunk of bread and flicked her an assessing glance. "That's right. How long did it take you to discover I was tracking you?"

"I sensed something after lunch but assumed it was someone from the tribe. Why didn't you call out to me?"

He thoughtfully rubbed his chin, shadowed with a day's growth of beard. "Do you want the truth?" Courtney nodded with pounding heart. Pushing aside his bowl and mug, he stretched full-length, lying on his side to face her, propping his head on one elbow. She thought he was like a sleek, black panther; even though he seemed satiated for the moment, she was still wary of him.

His eyes didn't leave her face as he spoke. "This morning I felt like I did when I was a boy—going off on a great adventure into the unknown. I hid behind a scrub palm and watched you paddle through the swamp mist. You made it seem so effortless. You reminded me of an Indian princess from an old storybook come to life, with your hair braided and falling over your shoulder.

"You seemed somehow magical in that canoe, gliding over the lilies. I felt that disturbing you would desecrate something sacred. If that makes sense." His voice sounded hoarse with some indefinable emotion.

Again, his words, the tone of his voice, baffled her. He sounded sincere . . . indeed, almost awestruck.

"I'm afraid I don't fit the part wearing jeans and worn-out running shoes," she said lightly.

"You know very well I'm not talking about the clothes. You're unique, Courtney. I noticed it the first time we were introduced at the firm. I'm only now beginning to understand why."

Her thoughts went back, remembering the instantaneous charge of excitement that had quickened her body when Silas said, "Courtney, this is my son, Jonas, who's just back from Washington. Stop whatever you're working on and leave it for the morning girls. Jonas has enough work to keep you busy indefinitely."

Courtney had looked up from the computer screen into a pair of green eyes so alive, so remarkable, she was lost. Jonas resembled his father in stature and mannerism but there the similarities ended. But that first meeting seemed a century ago, before she'd learned what he was capable of, she mused sadly.

She got to her feet, wanting to escape her thoughts. "I'll be back in a minute," she murmured and slipped out into the rain.

When she returned, her hair dripping, clothes damp, Jonas had put the food and dishes away for the night. She went immediately to her duffel bag and pulled out the mosquito netting. "Jonas," she said tentatively, "whatever your reasons for catching up with me, I thank God you did. I owe you my life."

The air crackled with tension. "Is that a Miccosukee custom? To be in the debt of the person who saves you?"

She spread the netting over both their bags to keep her hands from trembling. "It was a figure of speech."

"I'm sorry to hear that," he muttered. "I find the idea of your being in my debt rather stimulating."

"Please don't say things like that." She started to take off her shoes.

"Why? Because you're as disturbed by the idea as I am, in spite of your distaste for my way of life? Your lack of faith in me?"

Her hands stilled. She turned around and stared down at him. "Is that why you followed me? To seduce me in the forest and live out your fantasy before returning to the real world?"

His eyes glittered dangerously as he got to his feet. "I wanted to make love to you the first time we met. The office floor would have served my purpose equally well." He shifted his weight. "Now we have that point clarified, is there anything else you want to know?"

She swallowed hard. "I won't have an affair with you, Jonas."

"Did I ask you to?"

Her cheeks flamed with humiliation. "Why did you come?"

"Right now I'm wondering about it myself." On that icy note he shrugged into a windbreaker and left her standing there while he disappeared into the rain.

It seemed like hours instead of minutes before he came back. Taking advantage of his absence, Courtney quickly changed into an oversize T-shirt and undid the flap of her sleeping bag. She sprayed herself liberally with insect repellent, then climbed inside and lay facing away from him. She didn't dare extinguish the light. It would help him find his way back.

She feigned sleep when he returned. After making his own preparations for bed, he turned off the lantern. Once he'd settled in, all she could hear was the loud pounding of her heart over the rain drumming against the palm thatch.

The chickee floor was roughly nine by sixteen feet. All their gear and supplies didn't leave much room for his bag, which of necessity overlapped hers. It meant he was unbearably close.

Because he lay so still, she assumed he'd gone to sleep and that in turn made her even more restless as she struggled to find a comfortable position.

"Better say what's on your mind if either of us is going to get any sleep tonight," he muttered a few minutes later, gently tugging on her braid. Courtney felt his touch ripple through her body and sucked in her breath.

She spoke quickly. "When were you planning to tell me about your appointment to the Bureau? I had no idea you were willing to leave your law practice for something so... foreign."

She waited, but didn't dare turn around. "Jonas?" she prodded when he didn't answer.

"I phoned you from Washington to let you know an airline ticket was in the mail to you. But you'd already left the firm and I couldn't reach you at the apartment. I'd intended to give you the news in person the moment it became official." He paused and Courtney, too, remained silent. "Indian affairs have intrigued me since my law-school days," he went on. "After getting to know you and learning about your background, I had the mistaken notion the appointment would please you.''

Courtney buried her face in her arm, oddly pained by the revelation as well as the flat timbre of his voice. *How could he think she'd be pleased when they had no future and he was already committed to Laura?* Sick at heart, she tried moving farther away from him.

"Go to sleep, Courtney. It's been a long day."

"Good night," she whispered. For the second time they settled in their sleeping bags to the drone of the rain. Courtney suspected that she'd always feel strongly drawn to him and for the rest of her life would mourn the loss of something that could never possibly be.

Incredibly, she slept. When she awakened, she discovered Jonas preparing breakfast. At some point during the night the rain had stopped, and he'd taken down the tarps to allow the humid air to circulate. In fact, he'd already packed nearly everything into the kayak and the canoe.

The ham sizzling in the pan should have tempted her but she'd awakened with a splitting headache and felt slightly nauseated. On top of everything else, she'd had a nightmare reliving those moments with the alligator. If Jonas hadn't reached for her then and held her tightly in his arms for a few minutes, reassuring her in his low, familiar voice, she wouldn't have been able to fall asleep again.

Deep down she was thankful Jonas had insisted on accompanying her the rest of the way. Now that the shock had worn off, she was horrified by the events of the day before. He'd placed himself in mortal danger by coming to her rescue.

His voice startled her. "Are you ready to go?" he asked. "I don't like the look of those clouds."

Courtney followed his gaze. "It's going to rain later today, but we'll have reached Grandmother's before that. In any event, we've already covered the most hazardous part of the trip. Jonas, I have something to do first. If you don't mind, I'd like you to go ahead through that passageway on the right. It narrows to a thick path of water lilies like the one we crossed at the beginning. I'll catch up with you in a few minutes."

Jonas looked as if he wanted to say something, then thought better of it. His eyes searched hers, and she thought she saw a look of pain flit across his face before he nodded his dark head and walked to the shore. He adjusted the skirt of the kayak and paddled away, totally at home in the water.

She watched, silently admiring his skill until he disappeared, then she reached in the duffel bag for another change of clothes. Out of respect for her grandmother, she'd never appeared at her chickee in anything but Miccosukee clothing. Today could be no exception.

After quickly putting on the long, hand-sewn dress, Courtney unbraided her hair and brushed out the gleaming chestnut strands, which fell from a center part, rippling past her shoulders to her waist. A wry smile curved the corners of her mouth. Unmarried girls traditionally wore their hair loose and unadorned. Courtney was a little long in the tooth at twenty-six, but she still qualified as a maiden. She slipped on a pair of heavily beaded moccasins made by her mother and hurried down to the canoe with her duffel bag in hand.

The wind held steady and blew her hair behind her like a streaming banner as she pushed off and paddled steadily in Jonas's direction. A roseate spoonbill poked its head out from under a wet frond, as though watching to see if the coast was clear, then quickly darted away when it saw her.

Courtney paddled on, reaching the lilies beneath the protection of trees. But she saw no sign of Jonas. This part of the Glades was a prehistoric maze of cypress, red mangroves and hundreds of little ponds. Someone unfamiliar with the area could get lost and vanish without a trace.

Her heart started to hammer. "Jonas?" She waited but there was no response. "Jonas?" she called again, unable to disguise the panic in her voice as it reverberated in the stillness.

"I'm right behind you," he said in a deep voice. Forgetting the canoe, she stood up and whirled around, almost capsizing it. She didn't know who was more surprised. While she stared at the largemouth bass he'd just reeled in, he was staring at her as if he'd never seen her before.

"You look beautiful," he whispered reverently.

Her throat closed up. "My mother made it. She was an expert seamstress. The Miccosukee are renowned for their original patchwork designs. This dress is particularly elaborate because of all the bands."

The green of his eyes glowed incandescent. "The outfit is lovely, but I'm talking about the woman in the dress. I've been waiting to see you wear your hair unbound. It's magnificent. You ought to have a painting done against this kind of backdrop. I'd buy it and hang it in my library. Princess Suklatiki of the Glades."

"You remembered!" she cried out in surprise. She'd told him her Indian name once but had never dreamed it meant a thing to him. "Anyone seeing a painting like that would think you were mad, Jonas." Secretly his admission thrilled her.

"Bewitched, maybe," he said huskily, "but definitely not mad. Besides, how many people do you imagine I invite into my library?"

It was a question that caught her off-guard and one she didn't care to explore. Now was not the time to think about Laura, who would have the right to live with Jonas, the right to enter his favorite room, the right to his love....

She fastened her attention on the fish. "You've caught yourself a granddaddy. I wonder how many years it's been here. Wait till my grandmother sees it," she said, giving him a full, unguarded smile that made her eyes shine. For just a moment, the enmity between them seemed forgotten.

Unexpectedly his smile faded to be replaced by a sober expression. "Courtney? How long has it been since you last saw your grandmother?"

"Six months, more or less. Why?"

"Are you close?" He answered her with another question.

"Of course. In the Miccosukee tradition. Everyone honors and respects her. She's the matriarch of the family and her word is law."

Jonas was pensive. "Does she ever have contact with the outside world?"

All these questions puzzled Courtney. "If you mean does she ever leave the Glades, then no. But various people visit her from time to time. If you're concerned that she'll object to your presence, you have no need to be. When she hears how you saved me from the alligator, she'll say it was your destiny to be at my side at the precarious moment."

A thoughtful look entered his eyes. "I like the sound of your grandmother."

Courtney warmed to him even more. "Everyone in the family will enjoy meeting you, particularly as that fish will make delicious eating. And it'll provide conversation—my uncles and male cousins will want to hear how you caught it. So will my aunts and female cousins, but they'll pretend not to listen."

"So you think I'll be invited to stay for dinner?"

Courtney smiled. "Grandmother will insist on it." She tried to picture him through her grandmother's wise old eyes. She'd see a tall, strong, darkly handsome man, able to hunt and fish when necessary. A friend of her granddaughter's as well as a potential enemy because he belonged to a civilization she couldn't understand.

A shadow crossed Jonas's lean, intelligent face. "We'd better hurry."

Now that Jonas was with her, she felt no particular urgency to rush and reluctantly dragged her gaze from his body. This morning he wore a plaid shirt and jeans. A camera hung around his bronzed neck. She admired his deft movements as he stowed away his fishing gear and packed up the fish.

"Go ahead, Courtney. I'll follow."

This time she turned slowly in the canoe and sat down again. It was a strange but exhilarating experience to hear the dip of his paddle just behind her. She felt a kind of companionship she'd never known with anyone else, and certainly not here in the heart of the Glades.

They slowed down periodically when one of them spotted a marsh rabbit or deer. At one large pond they gazed in wonderment at a family of flamingos. Jonas snapped pictures of everything that intrigued him, then suddenly took one of her.

She looked away. "Don't waste your film on me."

"Why not? A snowy egret was in line just above your shoulder. It made a fabulous shot."

At Jonas's urging, they paddled on, stopping briefly at a stand of white mangroves a while later to drink from their canteens and eat some dried fruit. Then they set off again. Here the vegetation-choked water seemed to be a refuge for green turtles, perch and catfish. Courtney could hear Jonas's shouts of delight at everything he saw.

"We're almost there," she called out, imagining him as a young boy. From there her thoughts wandered to the sons he'd father one day.

"I gathered as much," he said paddling next to her, breaking her concentration. "Someone's coming, Courtney." He nodded in the direction of the hummock.

Courtney stopped paddling and got slowly to her feet. She called out a greeting in Miccosukee and a voice returned it. The sound caused some ibis to resettle in the myrtle bushes along the side of the pond. As the other canoe glided closer, Courtney recognized the man in it. "Jonas, meet Asiyaholo, one of my cousins."

Jonas nodded to the man, who was wearing a jacket and shirt in the colorful patterns of Courtney's dress. He wore his hair shaved except for a crest across his broad forehead. She could feel Jonas's eyes on the two of them, and assumed he was making comparisons.

"It's good you've come," said her cousin. "Grandmother died two days ago. Her body is resting where the lavender flowers grow."

Courtney was so stunned she couldn't speak. All she could think of was that she'd arrived too late. Though the family would never show emotion, because that was the Miccosukee way, Courtney had the blood of two races flowing through her veins. Her father had always been an open, affectionate man, who freely displayed his feelings. Courtney took after him in this respect and felt the tears well up in her eyes. They fell, unchecked, down her pale cheeks.

Automatically she turned to Jonas and recognized the compassion shining from his eyes. "You knew about Grandmother before we ever arrived here, didn't you? Who told you?"

He breathed heavily. "No one. A day or two ago I overheard Charlie the medicine man tell Bob that your grandmother wouldn't live to see the fall."

"He told me the same thing, but I thought there was still plenty of time to be with her." Courtney's voice trailed off.

"When I asked Bob if your grandmother had been ill, he said no, but that the medicine man was a seer. On an impulse I decided to come in case she was ill and you needed help. I'm deeply sorry she's gone, Courtney. I know how much you were looking forward to this visit."

The tears continued to stream from her eyes. Finally she had the truth from Jonas. In this case he had no other motive for coming than to offer comfort if she needed it.

"I'll leave now if you prefer it," he said, misinterpreting her silence.

As he made to turn his kayak about, she called out to him. "Don't go, Jonas."

His head swung around and his eyes blazed with light. "You mean that?" A pulse throbbed at the corner of his taut mouth.

She wiped away the tears with the back of her hand. "I'm glad you're here. Please stay unless you have to return to Red Mangrove right away."

"What do *you* think?" His tone was raw.

So many emotions stirred inside her, she almost didn't realize Asiyaholo was talking. He wanted to know if Jonas was the new superintendent. Word had reached the hummock that a white man was now in charge at Red Mangrove. She apologized for not explaining earlier who Jonas was, and they spoke for a few moments.

"Is something wrong, Courtney?" Jonas eyed both of them intently. "If I'm offending your family by being here, you need to tell me."

She hastened to assure him he was welcome. "They heard about the new appointment and wondered if you were the one. He says I must hurry if I want to see Grandmother before another storm hits. We'll follow him to the meadow."

"Does he mind that I'm tagging along?"

"Of course not. You're with me. He accepts that."

The three of them headed toward the cluster of chickees in the distance. Asiyaholo led the way while Courtney and Jonas paddled behind. She tried to imagine this moment without Jonas's comforting presence and couldn't. It frightened her how much she needed him. Right now it didn't seem to matter that he'd been the source of so much pain.

Her grandmother's family lived on a medium-sized hummock, full of lush plants and hardwood palms. Fifteen people had made their home there year-round and only occasionally ventured into the fringes of society. Now there were fourteen.

Everything seemed unreal as they pulled up to shore and got out of their boats. Asiyaholo said he'd share his chickee with another cousin so she and Jonas would have a place to sleep. Apparently Rosa had told Asiyaholo that Jonas was the special man in Courtney's life, and he took it as a matter of course that Courtney would want to be with him.

The camp appeared deserted, but the reason soon became obvious as they walked past several gardens and patches of berry bushes to a remote section of the hummock where lavender flowers bloomed in profusion. This was the place her grandmother had cherished.

The members of the family were dressed in clothes similar to Courtney's. They'd gathered to pay their respects and spoke only with their eyes as Courtney approached.

A fire burned at each end of the body, which had been laid across split logs with a small, thatched roof covering it.

Instinctively Courtney reached for Jonas's hand and felt his warm, strong fingers close over hers in a supportive grip. It broke all the rules of etiquette, since the Miccosukee didn't show feelings through physical gestures and touching, but Courtney had no compunction about clinging to Jonas.

Her family had learned to tolerate the strange white idiosyncrasies she brought with her. A long time ago she'd learned to cross the line between her two worlds and was equally at home in either. The transition was so simple she didn't have to think about it.

This time, however, she'd brought a white man with her. It seemed incredible that she was standing here, hand in hand with a stranger to the Glades, gazing on her grandmother for the last time. The old woman looked just the same to her now as she had when Courtney was a little girl. Shorter than Courtney, she'd grown stout like many Miccosukee women, but still retained her long hair, turned white as an egret's plume. The noble bone structure of her face was more pronounced in death, but she wore the look of peace.

Courtney let go of Jonas's hand to stoop and gather some blossoms, which she placed in her grandmother's hands. She gazed down at the familiar face, the lines now eased and softened, and identified traces of her own mother's lovely features. The loss of her grandmother brought back the sharp grief she'd suffered at her mother's death. Her mother, and now her grandmother—she didn't know if she could bear it.

She felt an urge to kiss her grandmother's brow but realized that on this sacred occasion it would offend the family. Jonas must have sensed her struggle, for he caught hold of her hand once more and grasped it tightly. She raised her face helplessly to his and discovered tears in his beautiful green eyes, almost as if he knew her heart. The moment moved her deeply.

The others would stay grouped around the body until the wind intensified, but Courtney had to go where she could give in to her grief in private. Jonas followed her lead and together they walked across the hummock, protected from the random gusts of wind by the stands of trees.

"If you'd like to be alone, I understand."

"No," Courtney whispered, "I need you."

CHAPTER FIVE

JONAS MADE A SOUND that might have been a soft groan. Releasing her hand, he enfolded her in his powerful arms. The gesture triggered something inside Courtney. She burrowed her face against his chest and broke down sobbing. He rocked her back and forth, murmuring endearments, letting her cry out her grief.

His hands smoothed the hair from her temples. "You've had too many shocks in the past twenty-four hours." Tenderly he kissed her eyelids. The contact released more emotion and she wept for a long, long time, unconsciously molding her body to his as she'd done so often in the past.

"Y-your shirt is soaking wet." She gulped back tears as she suddenly became aware of her surroundings and pulled away from him. But Jonas didn't let her go, not completely.

"Wet shirts seem to be a problem of mine."

A look of sweetness in his expression made her breath catch. She didn't know a man could look like that, let alone a man as dominant and male as Jonas.

Her drenched brown eyes gazed up at him through wet, inky black lashes. "Thank you for being here.

Thank you for saving my life yesterday. I'll never forget.''

He blinked. ''You sound like someone who's on the verge of saying goodbye. I thought you didn't want me to go,'' he murmured in a teasing voice. When he was like this, Courtney couldn't remember why he'd caused her world to collapse.

Calling on all her self-control, she moved out of his arms. He let her go with a grimace. ''It will be dark soon. I think we'd better bring our things up to Asiyaholo's hut, near that stand of slash pines.''

Jonas didn't say anything for a minute but slowly followed her down to the shore. Before long they had everything arranged as the night before. By the time the rest of the family returned to camp, Jonas had erected the tarps.

Courtney relieved him of the fish. ''I'll take this to the cooking hut and help with dinner. Feel free to walk anywhere on the hummock. It's not large and you can't get lost, but be back here within the hour.''

''I'd rather help you,'' he said in a quiet voice.

The intimacy between them threatened her composure. ''You've done your part by catching dinner. The women will do the rest.''

Jonas rubbed his neck. ''Well, since I'm superfluous around here, I guess I'll take a walk. Don't disappear on me now.'' He passed a finger beneath her softly rounded chin. His light touch was a reminder that it was weeks since she'd known the feel of his hands and mouth on her body. She immediately put distance between them.

"About a five-minute walk from here behind this hut you'll come to an open meadow, and beyond it you'll see the remains of a Calusa settlement. You might find it interesting."

"I'm sure I shall," he drawled. Something in his tone told her he was aware how much his touch disturbed her. Courtney had never been able to hide her response to him.

"In dry weather it's fascinating to look for artifacts."

"With a setting like this, no wonder your natural inclination when you started college was to turn to anthropology." He paused. "I realize you had no intention of telling me, but for what it's worth, congratulations on the grant."

On that note he walked away, leaving her more torn apart than ever. Why was he being so wonderful? She knew she was vulnerable to him right now, because of her grief. She knew, too, that she should guard against that weakness.

The downpour started as Jonas returned to camp. The family had already assembled in the cooking chickee, which had a palmetto log floor for seating and bare earth for the fire.

Courtney took charge of preparing the fish while her two aunts cooked hominy grits, sweet potatoes and biscuits made from the coontie plant. She shared with the others the mint-flavored coffee she'd brought for her grandmother.

They talked very little as they worked and were too polite to ask questions about Jonas. He appeared just as the oldest aunt heaped a pile of grits on the large *sofki,* or community spoon, and started to pass it around so each person assembled could eat from it, starting with the men.

Jonas's gaze sought out Courtney in the firelight. With a nod she indicated he should sit by her. "You don't have to eat from the *sofki* spoon, Jonas. It won't offend them," she whispered as the spoon was passed to him.

"I consider this a great honor, Courtney." He took the spoon from Asiyaholo and ate from it as he'd seen the others do. Then he passed it to Courtney, sending her a secret message with his eyes that said he was loving this.

She almost forgot to eat because once more she was touched by his reverence for her family's traditions. At this point she had to concede he was truly sincere in his interest and his respect for the tribe, if nothing else. She could understand why the tribal elders gravitated to Jonas. His behavior was not an act.

After the *sofki* spoon came the fish. "This is delicious," Jonas exclaimed. "What did you do to it?"

"I roasted it with limes."

"Is that the Miccosukee way?"

"No." She laughed softly. "It's mine. The Miccosukee way to too bland for my liking."

"It's a good thing your family can't understand what we're saying."

"Asiyaholo understands enough to talk to people when he comes to Red Mangrove. He wants to know how you caught such a big fish."

Jonas set down his coffee mug and looked across the circle at Courtney's cousin. "I used a fly rod and a popping bug. I cast it against the saw grass and popped it across the drop-off where a bass should have been, and right on cue there it was." When he finished, Courtney translated the difficult parts.

Asiyaholo smiled, a sight Courtney rarely witnessed, then spoke to her in Miccosukee. They conversed back and forth for a few minutes while the others kept their eyes straight ahead.

"Asiyaholo wants you to demonstrate this when he accompanies you as far as the hummock by the lagoon tomorrow on your trip back to Red Mangrove."

Jonas didn't say anything for a minute. "Is this your way of telling me I'm to leave in the morning?" He shot her a narrowed glance, and she knew she'd upset him. His abrupt change of mood had her heart pounding with shock.

"I assumed you'd have to be on your way. From what I know of a superintendent's job, you're always on call. And by morning the storm will have passed so you can be back there by dinnertime."

His eyes flashed. "Tell your cousin I'd consider it a privilege to go fishing with him, but in return, I'd like him to show me how to catch perch." His words were friendly enough but his manner was aloof throughout the rest of the meal, which ended with a dessert of wild grapes.

The men talked while the women cleaned up the kitchen. When Courtney had finished her share of the work, she walked over to Jonas, who was still sitting with the men. "You can go to the hut whenever you like. I'm going to help my cousin Solika put her baby to bed, and I don't know how long I'll be."

"If you expect I'll be asleep when you come to bed, forget it."

Courtney's face went hot. For once she didn't know what to say to such blunt talk and hurried to her cousin's chickee without a further word. She reached for the infant, who was swinging in a baby hammock next to his mother. For the next hour, she held the child, crooning to him softly, now and then exchanging a few desultory remarks with her cousin.

All the fires were extinguished and the camp was quiet when Courtney finally returned to their hut. Night was a time for sleeping in the Glades, particularly during a storm when there was no dry ground anywhere. Jonas trained a flashlight on her as she entered their chickee, trying to be as quiet as possible.

"Are you all right?" Jonas asked in a low voice before turning off the lantern.

"Yes." Instead of changing into a nightgown, she decided to sleep in her dress. Being fully clothed made her feel less vulnerable around Jonas. After crawling into her sleeping bag, she arranged the mosquito netting around the upper half of her body and sternly ordered herself to relax.

"I presume your relatives are grieving, but I can't tell from their stoic expressions," he whispered.

She sighed. "That's their way."

"If you want to cry some more, I've got a broad shoulder."

"Thank you, but I've cried my tears. I loved my grandmother and I'll miss her, but she'd lived a full life. The real tragedy lies in the fact that her history and memories died with her. I should have come sooner."

She could hear Jonas turn in his bag—he must be facing her back now, she thought. She could feel his warmth and prayed he wouldn't move any closer. "You had no way of knowing that her time had come. Still, I imagine your family can tell you many stories about your grandmother, maybe repeat some of the stories she used to tell."

"You're right," she whispered. What he said made perfect sense, but her emotions were still too near the surface for her to have any perspective. "I appreciate what you're saying. You're a very sensitive man. I realize they don't show it, but they have a favorable feeling toward you. You don't know what a compliment that is."

He shifted in his bag. "You mean you haven't enlightened them yet? I'm surprised."

Suddenly they were back on precarious ground. Her heart started to pound fiercely once again. "You're the new superintendent—they'll judge you on the basis of your actions. Look, Jonas. You literally saved my life and you've been very kind to me on this trip. Let's not get into an argument. Right now, the family accept you because you're my friend."

Angry laughter broke from him. "Do they have any idea that you're about as friendly as that alligator toying with you yesterday?"

"I wasn't toying with you, Jonas," she answered quietly.

"Like hell you weren't!" he ground out. Courtney flinched from the hostility in his voice and turned over in her bag to get up, but a hand shot out and captured her shoulder in a firm grip. "Where do you think you're going?" He'd raised himself on one elbow, bringing their faces closer together.

"I think it would be better if I go to bed in Solika's hut," she retorted, wriggling from his grasp.

"Oh no, you don't!" He suddenly grabbed her ankle and pulled her off-balance. She fell heavily across his lap, but before she could right herself, his hands tangled in her luxuriant hair, trapping her head so she couldn't move.

"How dare you!" She started pushing against his chest with her hands, but any movement on her part was checked by his powerful legs and body.

"How dare I what?" he whispered tormentingly. "Put my white man's hands on you and defile the sacred person? I'm going to do a lot more than that!"

In the inky darkness his mouth found hers with smothering force. Courtney gasped at the sheer violence of his emotions. He devoured her mouth with a raw savagery that swept aside all barriers. She couldn't elude him. No matter which way she turned he held her locked against him and continued to kiss her as if he were determined to draw the very life out of her.

"No, Jonas!" she begged as his mouth finally released hers long enough to travel over her face to her throat. There he pressed hot kisses against her scented skin. The feel of his lips sent shock waves through her body.

"You toyed with me, now it's my turn, don't you think?" In one lightning move he reversed their positions so she was half-lying on top of him with her arms crushed in his embrace. Ruthlessly he kissed her mouth, granting no respite, working a strange kind of magic that broke down her defenses. A few more minutes and she'd forget everything in the onslaught of his demands.

"Please—" she cried out, fighting for breath.

"What's the matter, Courtney? Are you fighting me or yourself? Tell me this isn't what you've been craving," he whispered against her skin. "Convince me this isn't what you've been missing."

Fearing he could sense that she was weakening, Courtney used all her strength to break away from his gasp. She stumbled to her feet and ran from the chickee, terrified that if he touched her now, she'd give in to her own desire to make love to him.

"Courtney?" Jonas called out in a frantic voice, but she ignored him. Tonight he'd caught her at a vulnerable moment. Her only recourse was to stay completely away from him and never get herself into this kind of impossible situation again.

The short run to the chickee in the rain drenched her clothes, so she borrowed one of Solika's nightdresses. She could wear something else in the morning until hers was dry.

As she lay down on the mat and pulled up the netting, the baby started to fuss. Grateful for the distraction, Courtney swung his hammock back and forth until he settled down again. Just now she'd give anything to trade places with him. No tormenting thoughts or dreams disturbed *his* sleep.

She curled up on her side, willing her heartache to subside. Her body throbbed from the sensations Jonas had brought to life. How would she be able to face him in the morning and pretend nothing had happened?

WHEN COURTNEY AWAKENED the next morning the rain had stopped and birdsong filled the hummock. Stretching, she sat up on the mat and met her cousin's look of surprise. Solika obviously wondered why Courtney had reappeared during the night, but she didn't ask. She merely smiled and continued to nurse her baby.

Courtney felt envy at the beautiful sight of mother and child so obviously contented and at peace. It seemed that Courtney's life had been in turmoil for a long time now. And worse, she had to go out and face the man responsible for it.

After a brief conversation with Solika, she dressed quickly in one of her cousin's garments and left the chickee. The inevitable pot of grits cooking over the fire indicated that she'd slept late. Had Jonas eaten breakfast with the others, or had he prepared something by himself?

She hoped he'd had a miserable night as she steeled herself for the ensuing confrontation. But halfway across camp she noted that the kayak was missing. She paused in mid-stride to scan the compound for signs of Asiyaholo, but he, too, had gone.

Her first thought should have been one of relief, but to her shock, a sense of loneliness, an emptiness too intense for examination, assailed her. Slowly she made her way to their chickee. All signs of Jonas had disappeared. She hardly knew where to turn next. It was then she saw the slip of paper weighted down by the stove and immediately recognized his bold, masculine script.

Courtney—I thought it best to leave as soon as the rain stopped this morning. Make sure someone accompanies you back to Red Mangrove when you're ready. Rest assured that you have nothing more to fear from me. Jonas

Tears pricked her eyes. She knew that his leaving was for the best—and apparently Jonas thought so too—but his words still hurt her deeply.

She couldn't help shuddering as she thought of the alligator. Would Jonas encounter it on the return trip? At least Asiyaholo would be with him as far as the lagoon. Courtney hoped her cousin would give him a description of the landmarks to watch for on his way back to the reservation. She'd intended to draw him a map, but it was too late now.

She walked to the edge of the camp and stared in the direction of Red Mangrove, praying Jonas would make it back safely. All their problems and difficulties didn't change the fact that Courtney was hopelessly in love with him. Despite her decision to never see him again, she couldn't imagine how she'd make it through the next month not knowing anything about him.

Asiyaholo didn't return until the next afternoon. Courtney had thrust herself into the family's daily routines and tried to fill the lonely hours with work, but the second she caught sight of his canoe rounding the bend, she raced down to the shore with pounding heart. Her cousin lifted his catch of bass high in the air and smiled at her. Courtney felt an immediate sense of relief, but she needed to know more. She began asking questions.

It seemed Jonas had given Asiyaholo his fly rod as a present. In return, her cousin had accompanied Jonas across the lagoon and set him on his way. Courtney sent up a prayer of thanksgiving, even though she knew that Jonas could always take care of himself.

She thanked Asiyaholo and took the fish from him. All the way to the cooking hut she could picture Jonas kayaking through the Glades. She glanced at her watch. He ought to be at Red Mangrove before long.

Throughout the rest of the day and night her thoughts were on Jonas—troubled thoughts. Except for last night's momentary aberration, Jonas had proved himself a caring, sensitive man with characteristics she had to admire. Courage, generosity, respect for her family... Somehow these qualities didn't add up to the kind of person whose actions she'd attacked so vehemently.

Nothing seemed to make sense anymore, and her contradictory feelings left her confused and frightened. She hoped that by the time she went back to the reservation she'd have herself well under control. Right now, a month without seeing him sounded more like an eternity.

FIVE WEEKS LATER the unmistakable sound of a helicopter hovering over the camp disturbed the early-morning birdsong. The noise sent Courtney flying out of her sleeping bag and running outside where she joined the other family members.

A helicopter in this area of the Everglades was a fairly rare occurrence, and she wondered how often her relatives had seen one. It bore the GSA insignia and immediately she knew it was Jonas.

Her heart hammered so hard she thought there might be something wrong with it as she struggled to get out of her nightgown and into her dress. The helicopter veered toward the open meadow and would land any minute.

In desperation she ran to her cousin Solika's hut for help. With her hands swathed in poultices from an accident the week before, Courtney couldn't possibly manage the buttons of her dress alone. She could just imagine what her long hair looked like. She'd spent another restless night of tossing and turning because of the burns on her hands. For the past week, the pain had nearly driven her mad. Despite the traditional herbal remedy, relief was slow in coming, and the pain had forced her to remain at the hummock longer than she'd planned.

She quickly explained to the family members that she thought it was Jonas in the helicopter so they wouldn't be alarmed, then hurried behind the hut to intercept him. She couldn't imagine why he'd come unless there was an emergency. Or unless Rosa had said something to worry him...

Courtney frowned as a troubling thought surfaced. *Perhaps her father was injured or ill.* Panic gave her a fresh burst of speed as she raced along the ancient footpath. Suddenly Jonas was there in front of her and, unable to stop, she collided with him. His strong hands shot out to grasp her upper arms in an effort to steady her, but the impact was hard enough to make her cry out in pain.

As he muttered an oath, Jonas's gaze darted to her hands, swathed in Miccosukee cloth. "So *this* is the reason you're so long overdue. I had visions of you tangling with that alligator, until I had to come and see for myself that you were all right." He broke off, staring into her upturned face, studying each feature as if he couldn't believe she was real.

Courtney had no way of knowing whether it was the pain or the sheer joy of seeing him again that made her feel weak and light-headed.

He looked leaner. There were shadows beneath his eyes as if he, too, hadn't been sleeping well. His black hair curled over his forehead and on his neck; she could tell he hadn't had a haircut for a long time. Most revealing of all, she detected a distinct pallor beneath that bronzed skin.

Slowly his hand slid down her arms to her wrists and he lifted them to inspect her hands. "What happened?" Whenever Jonas was upset, a pulse throbbed at his temple. It was throbbing now and Courtney tried hard not to stare. He'd asked her a question but she couldn't think with him this close, touching her.

"I—I did something stupid. I should have known better but I guess I've been away from the hummock too long and didn't remember."

"Remember what?" he urged, not letting her go.

"A friend in the Botany Department at the university asked me to gather plant samples the next time I visited the hummock. I had the canoe packed and everything ready for the return trip to Red Mangrove when I remembered his request. So I took another day to get what I could. I even had others help me.

"It wasn't until I noticed my hand blistering and turning black that I realized I'd come in contact with the poisonwood tree. Sap ran on my palms and burned them." She trembled as she felt the gentle caress of his thumbs, making lazy circles on her warm flesh.

"You need to see a doctor," he murmured.

Unable to bear his touch a second longer, she edged away from him, forcing him to relinquish his hold. "My cousins put herb poultices on the sores. They're much better today, actually."

"Did you bring any painkillers with you?" he asked, his keen eyes fastening on the shadows beneath hers.

"No." She shook her head and looked away. "I don't like the way they make me feel."

His dark brows furrowed. "How long have you been like this?"

"A week, but the pain isn't nearly as bad as it was."

His eyes were shuttered. "I'm taking you back with me now. Gill Travis, a pilot with the Bureau, flew me in. Tell us what needs to go and we'll start loading."

The thudding of her heart made if difficult to breathe. Once again he'd come to her rescue. Even though she'd treasured this time with her family, she had to admit it would be good to get back to Red Mangrove and her own home. And it might be another week before she could stand the friction of the paddle against her skin. But she was afraid to be around Jonas for fear he'd see how much he meant to her.

"I hate to put you out. Now that you know nothing's wrong, there's no need for your help. I'll be fine in—"

"Tommie's next hearing is in a few days," Jonas interrupted curtly. "He's decided he won't appear unless you're there. Under the circumstances, it's essential that you show up. I might have to use you for a character witness."

She'd forgotten about Tommie. Of course she couldn't let him down. But once the hearing was over, she'd make arrangements to visit her father, as she'd planned. She didn't dare stay at the reservation where there'd be the constant possibility of running into Jonas. If she had anything to be grateful for, it was that she wouldn't be alone with him on the return trip back to Red Mangrove.

"All right," she said in a low voice, unable to meet his eyes. "I'll inform the family." The tension between them was palpable. Jonas started to say something else, then apparently changed his mind and strode off angrily in the direction of the helicopter.

The next hour passed in a kind of blur, as Courtney let Jonas and the pilot take over while she said goodbye to her relatives. She realized it might be a long time, perhaps a year, before she could return. Asiyaholo agreed to tow her canoe back on his next trip to town.

"Where shall we put these?" Courtney whirled around at the sound of Jonas's voice. Her eyes took in several crates of provisions. He'd brought them for her family! There were oranges and grapefruit, coffee, powdered milk, salt, sugar, candy, everything one might think of for people far away from civilization. His thoughtfulness overwhelmed her and aroused her family's curiosity.

"I think the cooking chickee would be the best place," she murmured. Everyone gathered around when she called her relatives together to inform them of Jonas's thank-you gift.

At that point she witnessed something she'd never seen before. All fourteen of them smiled at him as Solika thanked him on their behalf.

Jonas smiled back, a full, unguarded smile Courtney hadn't seen for so long she'd almost forgotten how loved, how *privileged,* it used to make her feel. She had to look away.

A few minutes later Jonas assisted her into the helicopter. When she turned around to wave, she saw fourteen people sucking on lollipops, a picture she'd retain in her memory for all time.

Jonas strapped her into the seat behind him while Gill started the engine. The rotor blades screamed overhead and in seconds they were airborne. Courtney felt a wrench as she watched her precious family recede from view.

"Are you all right?" Jonas glanced over his shoulder, his green eyes not missing a detail of her tear-washed face. "You'll be visiting them again one of these days." His attempt to reassure her only made the tears fall harder and faster.

She cleared her throat. "That's not why I'm crying."

His black brows met. "You told me the pain in your hands wasn't as intense as before."

She shook her head in frustration. "Jonas, I'm crying because you made the family so happy. Your kindness will never be forgotten. Thank you for what you did."

His face closed into an expressionless mask. "I was simply trying to repay their hospitality to an uninvited guest. Your thanks aren't necessary."

Hoping that the pilot was too preoccupied to be aware of their conversation, Courtney stared out the window. They continued the journey in silence. Obviously things were now back to the way they were that night he'd visited her at Red Mangrove. It felt like an open wound that wouldn't heal.

She tried to concentrate on the flight. The sensation was quite different from flying in a large commercial airliner but she enjoyed it because she could see the Everglades at close range.

Deep in thought, she hadn't noticed that the helicopter was headed for Miami Beach until she saw the skyline appear on her right. "Where are we going?" she cried out in panic.

"Where do you think?" Jonas drawled, glancing over his shoulder.

"Jonas, we can't land at an airport with me looking like this! I thought you were taking me back to the reservation." After the isolation and quiet of the Glades, she wasn't ready for noisy crowds. And she couldn't tolerate the thought of strangers gawking at her unbound tangled hair and brightly bandaged hands.

"Come off it, Courtney. You're beautiful no matter what you're wearing, or how your hair looks. But if it'll make you feel better, I have a limousine waiting at the airport to take us directly to my house. Delia can help you bathe and dress while I call the doctor for an appointment."

Her first instinct was to demand that he take her back to the reservation, but with Gill Travis witness to everything, she had no desire to make a scene. As usual, Jonas had the upper hand. And he seemed to enjoy it, judging by the almost gloating expression on his face.

Courtney didn't want to be any more indebted to him. Why was he being so considerate? Was there a hidden motive for this display of kindness—apart from the fact that he wanted her help in court?

Soon Gill set them down at a heliport. True to Jonas's word, an elegant black Mercedes with smoked-glass windows was parked a few dozen yards away, waiting to whisk them to his home.

Jonas was out of his seat and assisting Courtney before the blades had stopped rotating. "Tell me what you need for the next few days. Gill will fly everything else back to the reservation. I've already talked to Rosa, who says she has a key to your place and will watch your things."

She'd always suspected that Jonas was the kind of person who planned ahead in case of an emergency. Nothing was left undone with him in charge. If she was honest with herself, she'd have to admit it felt wonderful to be taken care of for a change. And at this point, she was too tired from lack of sleep and too emotionally drained after seeing him again to take exception to any plans.

He jumped from the opening, then held out his arms and caught her by the waist, lowering her gently to the ground. She felt the warmth of his hands through the thin material of her dress and shivered from the brief contact.

"The small green duffel bag is all I need." It had several changes of clean clothes plus her cosmetics. Jonas released her to get her things, and she felt a sharp sense of loss. Five weeks away from him had left

This lovely Victorian pewter-finish miniature is perfect for displaying a treasured photograph. And it's yours FREE as added thanks for giving our Reader Service a try!

Harlequin Reader Service®   Sweepstakes Entry Form

This is your **unique** Sweepstakes Entry Number: 1W 626901

> This could be your lucky day! If you have the winning number, you could be the Grand Prize Winner. To be eligible, *affix Sweepstakes Entry Sticker here!* **(SEE OFFICIAL SWEEPSTAKES RULES IN BACK OF BOOK FOR DETAILS).**

> If you would like a chance to win the $25,000.00 prize, the $10,000.00 prize, or one of the many $5,000.00, $1,000.00, $250.00 or $10.00 prizes...plus the Mustang and the Hawaiian Vacation, *affix Prize Sticker here!*

> To receive free books and gifts with no obligation to buy, as explained on the opposite page, *affix the Free Books and Gifts Sticker here!*

Please enter me in the sweepstakes and, when the winner is drawn, tell me if I've won the $1,000,000.00 Grand Prize! Also tell me if I've won any other prize, including the car and the vacation prize. Please ship me the free books and gifts I've requested with sticker above. Entering the Sweepstakes costs me nothing and places me under no obligation to buy! (If you do not wish to receive free books and gifts, do not affix the FREE BOOKS and GIFTS sticker.)

316 CIH ACHR
(C-H-R-04/91)

YOUR NAME	PLEASE PRINT
ADDRESS	APT#
CITY	PROVINCE POSTAL CODE

Harlequin's "No Risk" Guarantee

- You're not required to buy a single book — ever!
- As a subscriber, you must be completely satisfied or you may cancel at any time by marking "cancel" on your statement or returning a shipment of books at our cost.
- The free books and gifts you receive are yours to keep.

If card is missing, write to: Harlequin Reader Service, P.O. Box 609, Fort Erie, Ontario L2A 5X3

Printed in U.S.A.

Business Reply Mail
No Postage Stamp
Necessary if Mailed
in Canada

Postage will be paid by

HARLEQUIN READER SERVICE®
P.O. BOX 609
FORT ERIE, ONTARIO
L2A 9Z9

Canada Post
Postes Canada
125

her hungering for his touch. Would the day ever come when she wasn't affected by his nearness? When she would feel nothing in his presence?

In the note he'd left at the chickee, he'd told her that she had nothing more to fear from him, and he'd meant it. While she'd been at her grandmother's he'd probably become officially engaged to Laura. Their wedding day couldn't be far off now. Between that and his job on the reservation—not to mention the campaign plans he was probably drafting—she marveled Jonas could still show this much concern for Tommie. Enough concern to come after Courtney to ensure she'd be in that courtroom.

He certainly hadn't flown to her grandmother's for any other reason. And once the hearing had concluded, their paths need never cross again.

Courtney should have been relieved at the prospect.

CHAPTER SIX

COURTNEY THANKED the pilot for all his trouble as Jonas ushered her to the limousine. She sank back against the upholstery and closed her eyes, savoring the coolness of the interior. Jonas joined her in the backseat and gave the driver instructions. Before she knew it, the car had passed the guard at the entrance to La Gorse Island, then drew up in front of the villa with its cool green courtyard dominated by a giant mango tree.

Delia, the housekeeper, hurried down the front steps and accompanied Courtney to the peach-colored guest bedroom she'd used on several other occasions. Much to Courtney's relief, Jonas stayed outside to speak to the gardener. Delia chattered enthusiastically, unaware of the underlying tension.

Delia helped remove the bandages, then Courtney entered the bathroom to enjoy a long, refreshing shower. Delia laid out fresh clothes for her and offered to help wash and braid her hair later.

. The amenities of civilization made a stark contrast to the lush greenery of the Everglades. The gleaming white marble floors and fixtures dazzled Courtney's eyes. Jonas's home possessed both comfort and a clean, understated elegance; she couldn't fault his taste. She was especially thankful for the air-conditioning. Even though she loved the Everglades, Courtney could stand the stifling humidity for only short periods of time. The icy cold felt like paradise. Not only was it invigorating, it made her less aware of the pain in her hands.

Much as she enjoyed the beauty and modesty of Miccosukee clothing, she had to admit that jeans and a blouse were more convenient. But the family expected her to wear the traditional dress, and she did so willingly whenever she visited.

She dipped in her cosmetics kit and found her favorite cologne, Fleurs de Rocaille. She hadn't worn any scent in the Glades because it attracted insects, but she had no worry now as she sprayed herself liberally.

"Come in," she called when she heard a knock on the bathroom door. But it was Jonas, not Delia, who appeared in the doorway.

He'd showered and changed into beige trousers and a pale blue cotton shirt that seemed to intensify his green eyes. "Delia's fixing lunch for us before I drive you over to the clinic. Let's get at that mane of yours, shall we?"

The thought of his hands in her hair thrilled her, but it terrified her more. "I'll wait for Delia," she answered quickly.

"We don't have time. The doctor's willing to fit you in as long as we get there before two."

There seemed no other choice but to let him help. Her hair was already wet from the shower and he poured a handful of rose-scented liquid onto the crown of her head. He massaged her scalp gently but thoroughly, working the shampoo into a lather, as if he'd been washing women's hair all his life.

"You have magic fingers," she whispered, almost melting from the sensation. Of necessity his chest brushed against her back and she felt the iron sinew of his legs against hers as he guided her head downward to rinse the flowing chestnut tresses in the sink.

"You smell divine," he whispered back. The warmth of his hard body combined with the scent of soap and the feel of his breath against her cheek began to play havoc with her senses. He had to know what his closeness was doing to her. Very soon she wouldn't be able to keep from begging him to make love to her. Her attraction to him was so strong she feared losing sight of her anger. His betrayal.

When she thought she couldn't bear his nearness another instant, he reached for a fluffy pink towel and began to dry her hair. The vigorous action helped to dispel the erotic tension, which seemed to have affected him, too, because he'd remained uncharacteristically silent.

"Turn around, Courtney." His husky voice gave him away as he picked up her hairbrush and began smoothing the long strands. The glazed look in his eyes reminded her of other moments when they hadn't been able to stay away from each other.

"Thank you, Jonas. I'll ask Delia to braid it later." She tried to move away but he grasped her elbows.

"Let me see your hands."

Sucking in her breath, she spread her open palms in front of him. The blackness had started to disappear and the burned areas were healing, but the injuries still needed attention.

His sensuous mouth tautened unpleasantly. "The sooner we get you to Dr. Johns, the better. Let's go,"

Delia had arranged lunch in the sun room, which overlooked the rectangular swimming pool on the west lawn. Courtney was ravenous and enjoyed every bit of the cold chicken salad. There were grapes and almonds tossed among the large chunks of white meat topped with a creamy ginger dressing.

Jonas offered her an orange roll. "You're thinner than the last time I saw you," he commented as he poured her a little white wine. "Why is that?"

She sipped it slowly, wondering what he'd say if she told him the same thing. Instead, she replied, "For the past five weeks we've eaten mostly venison for the evening meal because it's plentiful. I'm afraid I've never acquired a taste for it. You can't possibly imagine how delicious I find this lunch."

"I think I can. On one of my trips to China with the State Department we were detained a month and subsisted on local fare, which didn't taste nearly as good as deer meat."

Yet knowing Jonas, he'd never complain. He was the kind of man who could handle any situation and find some way to enjoy it. She'd never met another man to equal him. Resisting the trend of her thoughts, she stood up from the table abruptly.

"I'll ask Delia to braid my hair so we can go." Without waiting for his approval she fled from the sun room aware of his gaze on her long legs. She wished she had brought something more appropriate than jeans to wear to the clinic. But she hadn't counted on Jonas rescuing her and bringing her to Miami Beach, where she was virtually at his mercy.

While Delia braided her hair, Courtney vowed to herself that once the hearing was over she'd tie up the loose ends regarding her dissertation and leave for her visit to her father in Zaire. Seeing Jonas again was destroying the fragile defense she'd tried to build against his attraction.

The visit to Jonas's family doctor didn't take long. He prescribed an antibiotic for Courtney and sprayed a topical medicine on her palms to numb the pain, commenting that the herbal remedy had begun the healing process very effectively. After placing small gauze pads over the worst of the burns he prescribed a mild sedative to ensure her a good night's sleep.

Courtney and Jonas discussed Tommie's court case during the ride back to the house. Out of self-preservation, she shied away from topics that bordered on the personal. When they pulled to a stop in front of the villa, Courtney thanked Jonas for everything, keeping her words formal, her tone reserved, as she reached for the door handle.

"Where are you going in such a hurry?"

"To bed. I plan to take a pill and try to sleep around the clock." She didn't dare spend another minute in his company.

He rubbed the back of his neck. "I'll come up to your room later. If you're awake, I'll bring you a dinner tray."

His solicitude almost brought her to tears. "Please don't go to the trouble. I don't want my being here to interfere with your work anymore than it has already." Every time he went out of his way to make her comfortable, her longing for him grew more intense.

"I consider getting you better part of my work," was his terse comment before he supported her from the car. In the foyer he excused himself to go to his study.

Eyes glazed by fatigue, Courtney watched him walk away before she went to her room. She still couldn't understand why he was being so helpful and caring. Surely it wasn't just because of Tommie's case! But she shouldn't allow herself to speculate on his motives. Or his feelings....

It didn't take long for the sedative to work. Courtney slid between cool, silky sheets and knew nothing else until she awakened sometime after midnight with hunger gnawing at her stomach. If Jonas had brought her a tray earlier, she hadn't been aware of it. But now she was famished and knew she'd never get back to sleep until she had something to eat.

A white terry robe of Jonas's lay over the arm of one of the matching wicker chairs. He'd been thoughtful enough to leave it for her, probably guessing she didn't have one with her. She'd brought only the thin cotton nightgown she wore at the hummock. The aroma of the soap he used still lingered as she slipped the robe on and cinched the belt tightly around her slender waist.

Hoping everyone was asleep, she tiptoed barefoot out of the bedroom and made her way across the upstairs hall to the curving staircase. Running lightly downstairs, she headed toward the kitchen. All she needed was a piece of toast and a glass of milk or juice.

The moon was so bright she didn't have to turn on a light in the airy, modern kitchen and quickly found what she was looking for. As the toast popped up, Jonas suddenly walked in on her and switched on the overhead light. Blinking, she gasped in surprise. He was still dressed in his shirt and trousers.

His gaze wandered over her hair, disheveled from sleep, and studied her mouth, then settled on the toast. "I think we can do a little better than that!" He opened the refrigerator and pulled out mayonnaise, lettuce and a portion of roast, which he proceeded to slice before making her a sandwich.

"I'm sorry if I disturbed you."

"You didn't. I'm still working out some figures and came in here for coffee. How's the pain?"

She looked down at her hands so he couldn't see how his nearness affected her. "Until you mentioned it, I'd forgotten." She concentrated on the sandwich he'd placed in front of her, taking a large bite.

"I'm glad to hear it," he murmured as he efficiently prepared a pot of coffee. "You were out for the count when I looked in on you earlier." He handed her a banana from a bowl on the counter. "Here. I know you're starving."

"I am," she admitted, accepting it but avoiding his eyes. This close to him, with no one else about, she felt nervous and uncertain of herself.

He poured himself a cup of coffee, then leaned against the counter and eyed her over the brim as he drank. "Was your family able to help you write up your grandmother's history?"

She nodded. "I was amazed at the amount of information everyone contributed. In fact, I probably heard some details about her life with my grandfather she wouldn't have divulged herself."

"Like what?" His mouth quirked.

"Well—" her own lips curved upward "—the woman is the head of the family in Miccosukee culture because it's a matrilineal society, but occasionally Grandfather took charge. She didn't like it, so once, a few years after they married, he went hunting and didn't come back. She had to go after him and humble herself so he'd return to their chickee. It's a good thing she did or my mother would never have been born."

Jonas's eyes gleamed with quiet amusement and something else she couldn't quite decipher. "Your grandfather sounds like an intelligent man."

"I knew you'd say that," she said wryly. In the silence that followed, Courtney awkwardly peeled the banana and ate it, careful not to glance in his direction. The atmosphere had changed and she felt a heightened awareness of Jonas. At one-thirty in the morning, this was not the place for a conversation with him. Not when she could sense the strong undercurrents that aroused the passionate side of her nature, and his.

She put the peel down the disposal. "Thanks for the food. I think I can sleep now. Good night."

"Don't go," he murmured thickly as she started for the swinging door. Unbelievably she felt his hand reach out for her, sliding to the back of her neck. She couldn't leave.

"It's late," she whispered, hardly able to catch her breath.

"Do you really care?" His voice was husky now, urging her to stay. With his other hand, he began caressing her shoulders, finding the tight cords in her neck and upper back, massaging gently.

Courtney wanted to resist, fearing his power over her. But a yielding sense of delight began to spread through her body, swamping any attempt to fight him. She found herself submitting to the insistent pressure of his hands.

A low moan escaped as he kissed the tender nape of her neck while his hands moved sinuously down her hips and across her stomach.

"I knew if I touched you again, this would happen," he muttered in self-disgust, "but I can't seem to help myself. I want you, Courtney." He turned her in his arms and lowered his mouth over hers, kissing her until she couldn't draw breath. Without conscious thought she melted into him, caressing his back with her hands, reveling in his hardness and strength.

"I'm taking you to my room." In one swift action he lifted her into his arms, turned off the light and started for the foyer. Courtney delighted in being able to touch him like this again, to cover his face with soft kisses until he moaned with pleasure.

"If you keep on doing that, I won't be able to carry you upstairs," he warned, but Courtney couldn't seem to stop brushing her lips against the slight raspiness of his jaw and pressing kisses against his eyelids. "Courtney," he begged, his voice raw with emotion, and it was then she realized what she was doing. What she'd almost consented to do.

"I'm sorry," she whispered in panic, taking advantage of his momentary weakness to wriggle out of his arms and race up the stairs as if her life depended on it. With lightning speed he followed, grabbing hold of her wrist to prevent her from reaching her own bedroom.

"You're not running out on me this time," he vowed and practically dragged her across the upstairs hallway to the suite where he slept. But now she fought him.

"Oh, it's you, Jonas," a woman called out from a nearby doorway. "I thought I heard something." The sight of Delia in her dressing gown and night cream must have thrown Jonas off guard, because in that instant Courtney managed to break free of his grasp and dash to her room.

She heard their voices through the closed door but had no idea what they were saying. She could just imagine how Delia interpreted what she'd seen. Courtney should never have gone downstairs in the first place, she decided, then nothing like this would have happened.

Pulling off Jonas's robe, Courtney flung herself on the bed and willed herself to calm down. Her body throbbed from the sensations he'd aroused, and she doubted she'd be able to sleep, but she didn't dare take another pill.

Desperate to forget what she'd felt in his arms, she turned on the bedside light and took a paperback from her duffel bag but couldn't bring herself to open it.

A few minutes later she thought she heard a noise outside the door, although it might have been her imagination. For the greater part of the night she lay stiffly on one side, knees drawn up to her chest, waiting for oblivion to blot out the pain. She finally had her wish and didn't awaken until eleven the next morning.

Sunlight streamed in through the windows. Another hot, humid day without any sign of rain. Quickly Courtney stepped into the shower. After dressing in fresh shorts and blouse, she made her bed, then went downstairs to the kitchen, where she found Delia.

The housekeeper had the good manners—and the kindness—not to refer to the night before. She immediately prepared breakfast for Courtney and explained that Jonas had already eaten and gone to the reservation. He'd left instructions that Courtney was to do nothing but laze in the sun and eat. He'd also left a reminder that the court hearing was scheduled for the following day. Delia expected him back at dinner-time.

Courtney tried to hide her relief that she wouldn't have to face Jonas before evening. While she ate a breakfast of scones and sausage, she phoned her best friend, Linda, and made plans to have an early supper with her at their favorite restaurant. Linda's nursing shift would be over at four and then she'd be free.

After alerting Delia that she wouldn't be home until evening, Courtney phoned for a taxi and went downtown. She stopped at the bank, then went to an exclusive hair salon in Bal Harbour where even a trim cost a small fortune. But it was important to Courtney that her first haircut be done by an expert.

She'd kept her hair long out of respect for her mother and grandmother, one of the few traditions she'd maintained her whole life. But now that both of them were gone, Courtney couldn't wait to be free of her unruly mane.

The hairdresser spent an hour with her discussing various styles. Eventually Courtney left the salon feeling pounds lighter. The softly layered hair now brushed her shoulders and fell from a side part with feathered bangs that had a slightly windblown look. It felt natural, and everyone in the salon said it emphasized her exotic eyes and softly sculptured mouth.

The new hairstyle called for a new dress and different makeup, and Courtney headed out purposefully to do something about that. When she waltzed into Luigi's hours later, Linda didn't recognize the elegant-looking model-thin woman wearing a summery green-and-white-print dress with apple-green high heels and lipstick in a stunning coral shade.

"Linda?"

"I don't believe it!" her petite blond friend gasped when she realized it was Courtney. The transformation appeared to be total. "You were always the most beautiful girl at school, but now you're gorgeous! I'm so jealous I could croak. What's *happened* to you?" she cried out incredulously.

Courtney averted her eyes. *Jonas had happened to her.* She could still remember the feel of his hands and his body as he washed her long hair. How could she have been so foolish as to believe that in cutting it, she could destroy that memory? "Why don't we order our meal and I'll tell you."

"Did Jonas ever catch up with you?" Linda zeroed in on the essentials the minute they were seated. Courtney nodded and pretended interest in the menu. "All right, my friend," Linda insisted. "Out with it. I want to know everything and I mean *everything!*"

Courtney started to chuckle and put the menu back on the table. She didn't really need it since she always ordered cannelloni.

Linda's blue eyes fastened on her in rapt attention. The women gazed at each other briefly, but it was Linda who spoke first. "You're in love with him."

"Yes," Courtney whispered, in a trembling voice.

"You're getting married. Right! And I'm to be your maid of honor."

"No." Courtney couldn't hold back the tears that filled her eyes.

"What's wrong, Courtney?"

"Oh, Linda..." She broke down and for a few minutes couldn't talk. She was finally able to regain control of herself and told Linda what had happened at the law office, as well as the terrible confrontation with Jonas at her place on the reservation.

After Courtney had finished, Linda eyed her for a long moment. "The man's crazy about you. I'm sure of it. If he told you his father and Laura were lying, then you should have believed him. Aside from the cases he was obliged to discuss with Laura over a business lunch or dinner, did he ever give any indication that he was romantically involved with her?"

"No." Courtney shook her head.

"Well, then?"

"Linda, you would've had to be there when Silas made his announcement. There wouldn't have been any doubt in your mind either, believe me." Her voice shook with remembered pain.

"Didn't you find it odd, not to mention in extremely bad taste, for his *father* to be the one breaking news like that? Especially with Jonas nowhere around? Surely an announcement that important was Jonas's prerogative, no one else's. Certainly not his father's. Besides, didn't you tell me he and his father weren't on the best of terms?"

"Yes."

"I'm beginning to see why. Courtney, how would you like it if your father took matters into his own hands and announced something of a private nature concerning you to a room full of people? Particularly if it wasn't the truth?"

Courtney blinked as the import of Linda's questions sank in. "I'd be furious. But Linda, Silas adores Jonas. Why would he purposely lie like that? It could cause him to lose Jonas completely."

Linda cocked her head to the side. "I don't know. Wishful thinking, perhaps? Maybe he's living out his own frustrated ambitions through Jonas. Perhaps Silas needs to feel important and gets mileage just from being his father. Jonas is a remarkable man, Courtney. One in a million."

"I know," Courtney said in an agonized whisper.

"A man like that would never allow anyone else to dictate his destiny, or—" she paused significantly "—choose his wife for him. Think about it."

Courtney stared down at her food without seeing it. "I am thinking. But Laura told Ray—"

"Come on, Courtney!" Linda flashed her a knowing glance. "If Jonas had wanted to marry Laura, he'd have done it ages ago. I thought you told me she'd been with the firm five or six years."

"That's what Silas said."

Linda sighed. "If I were you, I'd be inclined to trust Jonas when he said it was all fabrication. It could explain why he's made a total break with the firm. Can you think of a more perfect way for Jonas to remove himself from their schemes than by becoming a superintendent?"

"E-even if what you've said is true and Silas lied, I'm not convinced Jonas accepted the appointment for those reasons, Linda. He admitted he'd once considered going into politics. I'm not so sure that isn't still in the back of his mind."

Linda leaned forward and put a placating hand on Courtney's arm. "Would that be so terrible? I don't understand you. It's not a crime to run for governor."

"No, of course it isn't. It's Jonas's motives for getting involved with me that I question."

"Courtney—" Linda cried out in exasperation. "What other reason would he have for spending every waking moment with you if he didn't love you?"

"I can think of several. In an effort to win votes, he's decided to woo the groups most interested in saving the Glades. Befriending the Indian population is part of his plan. When he met me at the office, he saw a golden opportunity to tap a resource that had been handed to him. Silas even thanked me in front of everyone for helping smooth the way for Jonas with my mother's people."

"I don't believe what I'm hearing." Linda shook her head. "You just got through telling me the tribe asked Jonas to be their superintendent as far back as a year ago, before you ever went to work at the firm. Think!"

"But he didn't accept the appointment until he'd been seeing *me* for a couple of months, plying me with questions, learning everything he could about reservation life. He was so interested in me and my background, I foolishly thought it meant something else." Her voice trailed off.

"You don't know that it didn't."

"I do," Courtney shot back. "Jonas never proposed marriage to me. Let's be honest, Linda. Can you see me as Mrs. Jonas Payne, wife of the governor of the Sunshine State? I can assure you he can't, either. But he wouldn't be averse to an affair on the side. I know he wants me. He's never lied about that. But his business dealings are another matter. He's not above taking advantage of the tribe as a source of funding for his campaign. I have proof of that."

It was Linda's turn to blink. "Have you confronted Jonas with this proof?"

"Yes. He admitted that he kept a substantial amount of the twenty-million-dollar settlement for a project he was working on."

"But did he tell you it was for his campaign?" she persisted.

"No."

"Why didn't you press him for a definitive answer?"

"Because I didn't need to."

"Then how do you know anything for certain?"

She moistened her lips. "I don't, but after what Raynor told Laura, there's no doubt in my mind."

"But we've already established there's a conspiracy going on behind Jonas's back at the firm."

"Raynor had no idea I could hear him. He was having a private talk with Laura as I was leaving. I didn't mean to overhear them."

A long silence stretched between them. "Courtney, since I'm your best friend, I'm going to tell you something for your own good, even if you don't want to hear it."

Courtney averted her eyes, heartsick and confused.

"I think you're making a big mistake allowing yourself to be influenced by other people. Why not go to Jonas and ask for the truth? From everything I know about him, he's anything but a grasping, opportunistic monster. Look what he did for you, flying you out of the interior and getting you to a doctor. He even brought gifts for your family when he didn't need to. I tell you, if someone like Jonas ever came into my life, I'd grab him so fast your head would spin."

Courtney raised her pain-filled eyes to meet Linda's. "You make it sound so simple and straightforward, but it isn't."

"I realize that. Forgive me for speaking my mind, but I hate to see you so unhappy."

"There's nothing to forgive. I've needed this talk," she said with a tremor in her voice. "Since we were girls, you've been like a sister. It's meant a lot to me."

Linda wiped the edge of her mouth with a napkin. "Under the circumstances I think we ought to get out of here and go to a movie. There's a new comedy playing down the street. How about it?"

The idea appealed, if only because it would keep Courtney away from Jonas for a few more hours. Talking to Linda about him had deepened Courtney's anguish over an impossible situation.

Two hours of comic relief proved to be the tonic Courtney needed. When Linda drove her back to Jonas's house at ten that night, Courtney felt pleasantly tired and in control of her emotions. She gave Linda a hug, promising to call her in a couple of days. Then she hurried up the front steps, clutching her purchases, to let herself in. Naturally the door was locked.

As her finger went to the bell, the heavy wooden door was suddenly flung open. Jonas stood there still in work clothes, looking like a avenging angel. His face was white with fury and his green eyes narrowed to mere slits.

Automatically Courtney's hand flew to her throat as his attention fastened on her hair. For the longest time he didn't say anything, but unlike the admiring glances she'd received from men throughout the evening, in Jonas's eyes she saw only anger.

"I guess I don't have to ask where you've been." He stood aside so she could pass, then shut the door and leaned against it, strong bronzed arms folded across his broad chest. She heard him mutter beneath his breath. "Why did you do it?"

She knew exactly what he meant, recalling the sensuous experience of the night before when she'd felt his hand in her hair. "Why does any woman change her hairstyle from time to time?" She couldn't explain that cutting her hair had been in part a reaction to that momentary lapse when she'd let down her guard.

"You're not *any* woman," he said thickly. "You don't resemble Princess Suklatiki anymore."

He was back to that again—but why? "A man doesn't have any conception what it's like to deal with long hair on a day-to-day basis."

"What's this all about, Courtney? Off with the old and on with who knows what?" he lashed out. "I have the feeling your mother would turn over in her grave if she saw you like this."

His words kindled her anger because they touched a nerve. "And I wasn't aware that staying in your home as a guest for a few days meant I had to have your permission to live my life as I see fit."

He straightened and his hands formed into fists at his sides. "It's because I've been in *your* home that I said anything at all. Asiyaholo won't know who you are the next time he comes to Red Mangrove." His thunderous tone expressed total disapproval.

Her chin lifted. "I'll be in Oklahoma before he makes another trip."

"Turning your back on your mother's people so soon?" He knew exactly where and how to hurt her.

Her nails dug into her palms but she barely noticed the pain. "That was cruel, Jonas. What I do with my life happens to be none of your business."

A stony-faced stranger stood before her. "Shall I tell that to Tommie in the morning?"

She held her ground. "I'm planning to be there tomorrow morning, unless you've changed your mind. Otherwise I'd—"

"Otherwise you'd have run off again." The contempt in his tone hurt more than she would have thought possible. "Go ahead and run, Courtney. No one's chasing you this time. As far as I'm concerned, you're as dead as that host tree we passed in the Glades."

She could picture the exact tree he meant and shuddered. "What time do we need to leave for court in the morning?" She made an effort to keep her voice steady and dispassionate.

"Eight-thirty."

"I'll be ready."

"Don't be surprised if Tommie closes up tighter than a drum when he sees you. I don't suppose it occurred to you to wait a day before taking on your new persona."

In actuality, Courtney hadn't thought beyond cutting all ties with Jonas, emotional as well as physical. A change in hairstyle had seemed a fitting way to begin a new life, one that didn't include him. She hadn't considered that cutting her hair might be construed as a sign forsaking her Miccosukee heritage. The fact that it had taken Jonas to point it out to her made her pain even more unbearable.

"Unless you have something else to say regarding Tommie's case, I'm going upstairs." She swept past him and managed to make it to the guest room before crumpling in a heap on the bed.

CHAPTER SEVEN

THE SECOND the judge pronounced Tommie innocent and dismissed the case, Courtney approached the chief. "May I drive back to the reservation with you and Tommie? There's something I'd like to discuss with you."

"You're not traveling with Jonas?"

"No." She knew Jonas was planning to take her back to his place, but while he was detained in the judge's chambers for a few minutes, she decided to make her escape.

"Sure. Come on."

The three of them left the courthouse and walked the short distance to the truck. Courtney breathed a sigh of relief when they turned the corner and headed into the mainstream of traffic. Jonas would probably be glad when he found she'd left without him. He could always bring her duffel bag the next time he came to the reservation.

"What's on your mind, Courtney?"

She bit her lip. Ever since her talk with Linda, Courtney had decided to take her friend's advice and try to find out the truth about Jonas. "I know you're grateful to Jonas for everything he's done for the tribe, and for you and Tommie, personally. But how well do you really know him? Do you trust him implicitly?''

Bob didn't say anything; neither did Tommie. Sometimes the chief could be stubborn, and this was one of those times. The men stuck together.

''It's true that Jonas won a huge settlement for the tribe in Washington, but I understand he's retaining a great deal of the money for a personal project and I wondered what you thought about that.''

Still there was no response from the chief.

''Aren't you worried he might be taking unfair advantage of the situation?'' she asked in exasperation.

The chief made a funny noise. ''The tribal council knows what's going on, Courtney. These matters are best left to the elders.'' With that succinct comment, he put her firmly in her place.

None of them talked for the rest of the journey to Red Mangrove. But when the chief pulled to a stop in front of Courtney's place to let her out, he said, ''You're just like your mother.''

Courtney realized she could take that statement any number of ways. ''You mean I'm too outspoken?''

''No. Paranoid.''

Paranoid? Courtney couldn't believe he'd said that to her!

''Thanks for your help,'' Tommie said shyly in Miccosukee.

''Anytime, Tommie,'' she answered in the same language.

''See you later, Courtney. Thanks for helping Tommie,'' Bob said before starting the engine again.

"Thank you for the ride," she called after him.

His remark still rankled as she let herself into the house. She found herself thinking about it as she unpacked the things brought back in the helicopter from her grandmother's hummock. Later that night when she finally fell into bed exhausted, she was still pondering the chief's comment.

It forced Courtney to consider her mother in a different light, for the first time. Had her mother's independence been a cover for fears she hadn't been able to overcome? Was that why her marriage failed?

The thought continued to trouble Courtney, and as a result she slept poorly. Awakening the next morning, she decided to ask her father about it on her upcoming visit.

After Courtney had showered and dressed, she gathered up some baskets and dolls made by her family and walked over to the local store. To her astonishment it wasn't open. In fact, looking around, she noticed that the town seemed positively deserted.

Puzzled, she hurried to the restaurant and went inside. "Rosa? Where is everybody? I wanted to leave this stuff at the store, but no one's there!"

Rosa stared hard at Courtney and obviously didn't like what she saw. "If you ever stayed around here long enough, you'd know what's going on," the older woman chided. Rosa wasn't one to make a secret of something she didn't like, and she didn't like Courtney's new hairstyle, but she'd never come right out and say it.

Privately, Courtney had to admit she'd felt like an outcast since she'd cut it. Even Bob had averted his eyes when he first saw her and had exhibited a coolness even after she appeared on the witness stand to vouch for Tommie. True to Jonas's prediction, Tommie had hung his head as if he were embarrassed.

As for Jonas, once when she ventured a glance in his direction, she'd captured a disdainful look that said, "I told you so."

"Well, I'm here now," Courtney teased, trying to cajole the older woman out of a bad mood.

Rosa only grunted and went on mixing her famous pumpkin bread behind the counter. "Now that your grandmother's gone, I guess we won't be seeing you here as often."

Courtney froze. "Who told you that?"

"People."

She bristled. It meant that Jonas had been discussing her with Rosa.

"Is it true?" Rosa asked point-blank.

"No. After I finish in Oklahoma, I'll be teaching in Miami. You'll see me most every weekend."

Rosa shook her head. "Once you leave the state, you'll never come back. That's what happens. Your mother wouldn't like it, you know."

Courtney groaned in frustration. She simply couldn't make Rosa understand. "Mother gave me to Daddy so I could find my place in white society and earn a decent living. But that doesn't mean I don't love my home here."

"She made a mistake."

"That's your opinion, Rosa. What you don't understand is that anthropology is my life's work, just as the restaurant is yours."

"Not for long, it isn't." She stopped her bread-making long enough to serve Courtney her usual roll and glass of juice.

"Now you're being mysterious," Courtney murmured. "Have you decided to marry Eddie and live on the Trail?" Eddie had wanted Rosa since her first husband died.

"Eddie can wait. I'm going to become financially independent first."

"And how are you going to do that?" Courtney asked as she munched on her hot cross bun.

"I'm going into the cattle business."

For a minute Courtney was sure she hadn't heard Rosa correctly. "Does that mean you're moving to Montana?" she quipped playfully, but Rosa's mouth remained stubbornly set.

"I'm staying right here where I belong."

"To raise cattle."

"That's right. I already own two hundred head of Angus."

Choking on her roll, Courtney grabbed for her juice. "You what?"

"You heard me. Everyone on Red Mangrove owns cattle now."

"Since when?"

"Since three weeks ago."

"What happened three weeks ago?" Talking to Rosa was like talking to Bob Willie. They never gave her the whole picture of anything. She had to drag it out of them bit by bit until it drove her crazy.

"The council voted to buy cattle."

"But how could they? That costs hundreds of thousands of dollars!"

"That's right."

"But we don't have that kind of money."

"We do now."

At this point Courtney was on her feet, the rest of her breakfast forgotten. "No one on this reservation knows anything about raising beef cattle."

"Jonas does."

"I knew it!" Courtney whispered, white-faced.

"What are you so mad about? You don't care what goes on here. You'll be leaving soon."

"That's not the issue, Rosa."

"If you don't live here, then you don't have the right to voice an opinion."

"I haven't left yet!"

"You've changed. It's the same thing," Rosa went on with dogged determination.

"Because I cut my hair?"

"Your mother would never have allowed it."

"Why do you continually forget that I have a white father?" she asked heatedly.

"Huh!" Rosa snorted. "As if I could forget. You look like him all right, but *he* respected our ways."

"And he and Mother were forced to live off the reservation."

"Nobody's forcing *you* to go away, Courtney." Rosa's coal-black eyes pierced Courtney. She and Rosa had reached an impasse for the moment.

"Would you be kind enough to tell me where everyone is?" Courtney asked tightly.

"Jonas and the chief are holding a meeting with some men from the Cattlemen's Association over at the schoolhouse. He's already met with the women. We're having classes in cattle management."

"Tell me you're joking." Courtney was stunned.

"Two hundred head of cattle for each member of the reservation is no joking matter. That tribal land settlement was used to fund this project. Jonas and the elders have been working on the plans for more than a year. In time it's going to make the tribe real money!"

"Where are you going to keep the cattle?"

"On the land won back from the government, of course."

Courtney felt the blood drain from her face. *Was this the project Jonas had referred to?* Suddenly Courtney felt ill and dropped the armful of dolls and basket she was holding.

Rosa eyed her steadily. "What's the matter with you? You look like you just saw a bad spirit."

Courtney couldn't speak and dashed out of Rosa's place, leaving the fallen articles behind. She had to find Jonas! Anxiety tied her stomach in knots as she approached the schoolhouse, where at least fifty men from the reservation were assembled.

Not wanting to disturb them, she stood in the back of the auditorium and listened to a man knowledgeable in animal husbandry. He was explaining things through the use of a translator. Jonas sat behind the podium next to Bob Willie and another man she'd never seen before.

An hour went by before the meeting broke up. If Jonas saw her, he made no move to acknowledge her presence. She'd have to seek him out, but feared his rejection. After having disappeared from the courtroom without saying a word to him following Tommie's court case, she couldn't imagine what kind of reception she'd get now.

One by one the men filed past Courtney, averting their eyes as they left the auditorium. Calling on inner courage, she made her way to the front of the room and waited until Jonas finished talking with one of his guests to flash her a contemptuous glance.

"Jonas? May I speak to you for a minute?"

"If you have a question to ask these gentlemen, I suggest you attend the next scheduled meeting for the women."

The blond-bearded man he'd been speaking with looked as if he was willing to entertain any questions she had. "It's all right, Jonas." He smiled at Courtney, as did the other man. They both acted more interested in her than in the discussion they'd been having, but their flattering attention only seemed to infuriate Jonas. His icy stare caused a tight band to constrict around her chest so she could hardly breathe.

"Jonas." Her eyes pleaded. "I was hoping to speak to you before you left today."

"Is it tribal business?" he asked with brusqueness that shocked her.

"In a way," she offered lamely.

"Excuse me a moment," he muttered to the men, grasping Courtney's elbow to maneuver her out of earshot. "Say what you have to say. You have exactly one minute." He let go of her arm as if it scalded him.

She bit her lip. He was too unapproachable for any kind of conversation, and his nearness only distracted her. "I might need a little longer than that."

"As you can see, I'm busy. Take it up with Bob."

She ran trembling hand through her bangs. "*You're* the only one who can answer my questions."

His lips thinned. "Then call my secretary and make an appointment."

She rocked back on her heels. "Are you being deliberately obstinate or just plain rude?"

"I believe you've garnered those honors hands down, Courtney. Your minute is up."

"Jonas—" she whispered in agony, "please don't be like this. I need to talk to you."

There was an interminable silence. "As I told you, get in touch with my secretary. My office number is posted on the bulletin board at Rosa's place. Now I have to go." He strode back to the men without a backward glance.

Courtney slipped out of the auditorium and headed for Rosa's. She ignored the older woman's inquiring stare as she looked at all the announcements on the bulletin board. Sure enough, Jonas's business address and phone number were listed. Apparently he'd opened up an office in Miami rather than Miami Beach. By the address she guessed it was a far cry from the Payne law firm at Bal Harbour.

The poster stated that anyone on the reservation who needed to reach him could call toll-free, day or night. Courtney certainly needed answers to a few questions or she'd never have a moment's peace again.

Without explaining herself, she asked Rosa for a pencil and paper and jotted down the information, then called for an appointment on the restaurant phone.

At three the next afternoon she was waiting in the reception room of Jonas's office. "Mr. Payne will see you now," said the pert brunette receptionist after informing Jonas of Courtney's arrival. For a moment, Courtney felt jealous. A secretary shared a relationship with her boss that was not unlike a wife's. Courtney hated the idea that another woman had the right to his full attention. Even if it was in an official capacity, relationships could change and often did. Her own relationship with Jonas attested to that.

Courtney walked past the woman's desk and entered Jonas's office. It was a simple room with a desk and three chairs. A place that would never intimidate. A place where members of the reservation would feel comfortable. It was perfect for the kind of job he had to do.

Jonas sat back in his swivel chair dressed in a khaki-colored shirt. The dull green made a striking foil for his bronzed skin and black hair. He'd managed to fit in a haircut since the hearing, but no matter how he wore his hair, he was the most attractive male she'd ever met in her life.

"Thank you for seeing me, Jonas," she began and sat down in one of the metal folding chairs opposite his desk. His mocking glance told her to get straight to the point. "Would you answer me one question?"

He chewed on the end of his pen. "That depends."

Obviously he had no intention of making this easy for her. She honestly couldn't blame him after everything that had happened.

"Is this cattle project the project you were referring to when I asked you about the settlement?"

He watched her steadily. "That's right. Bob and I have been discussing the feasibility of running cattle on the reservation in the hope that it will become a viable business for the tribe. The land belonged to the Miccosukee and was illegally taken from them years ago. Now it's theirs again."

A wave of dizziness assailed her. "And you purchased cattle with the profits?" The question was purely rhetorical because she knew the answer already.

"Some of the profits were invested. The council is planning to build a new hospital on the reservation, but that's still down the road."

She couldn't remain seated. "Jonas—" She clung to the edge of his desk for support. "I had no idea." Her eyes searched his face. "Why didn't you ever tell me about any of this when we were seeing each other?"

His expression was remote. "As close as we were at that time, I didn't have permission from the council to discuss the matter with anyone, not even you. They retained me to perform a service, and I was under covenant to keep their plans confidential. I would have lost their trust by divulging their business to anyone else."

He was speaking the truth. Courtney knew that. And because Jonas was an honorable man, he'd gained the admiration and respect of every member of the tribe.

"What you've done could revolutionize life on the reservation," she said, not hiding her own admiration. "I'm deeply ashamed for having misjudged you. I can only tell you I'm sorry and hope you'll be able to forgive me."

"Apology accepted," he said stoically. "But it's early days yet, Courtney. Only time will tell if this idea will prove more productive than others have in the past."

"The only reason for it not to work will be if you step down and give the responsibility to someone else who doesn't have your knowledge and ability."

He sat forward, his facial muscles tight. "Either I'm a man grasping for every opportunity he can get, or I'm an expert with vision. Which is it, Courtney? You can't have it both ways."

Her face went hot. "I know now that I was wrong about you and you have every right to despise me. But what I'm trying to say is that I hope you'll stay with this program long enough to make it really work!''

He rose slowly to his feet. ''Am I going somewhere?'' he asked in a dangerously soft voice. ''You have this amazing facility for reading my mind and understanding my plans better than I understand them myself.''

She took a deep breath. ''Does Bob Willie know the position of superintendent might only be a stopgap?''

''Stopgap for what?'' he hissed in such lethal tones she backed a step or two away from the desk.

''Jonas—I know the background you come from. Though you may not be interested right now, there's a real possibility that sometime in the near future you'll change your mind and decide to enter politics. It would be a tragedy to see the cattle program fail just when the tribe has started to follow your lead. My mother's people need someone who'll be there for them through a lifetime. It's the only way a new idea like this will ever grab hold and work.''

To her surprise, he sat there without any expression on his face. It seemed like hours before he said anything. ''If you came to apologize, consider it done. Now, I have other business to attend to. I believe you know your way out.'' He buzzed his secretary. ''Send in my next appointment, Cindy, then we'll go to dinner.''

Courtney had been well and truly dismissed. ''Goodbye, Jonas,'' she whispered, her throat aching with suppressed emotion. She nearly stumbled trying to get out of his office without making a complete fool of herself.

It was after nine that night when Courtney pulled up in front of her house on the reservation and hurried inside, where she could finally give way to her despair in private. She should never have gone to Jonas's office. It had only made things worse, if that was possible.

She jumped when she heard a knock at the front door. Ridiculous as it was, she thought it might be Jonas and ran across the room in feverish anticipation. "Rosa!"

"You were expecting someone else maybe?"

Courtney ran shaky hands through her hair. "No, of course not. Come in."

Rosa stayed where she was. "No, it's late. I'm tired and from the looks of you, you should have been in bed a long time ago. Bob Willie sent me."

"What is it?"

"The tribal council has decided Jonas can attend the Green Corn Dance, but he'll need an interpreter. Bob wants you to do it."

Courtney stared hard at Rosa. "Outsiders haven't attended that ceremony in years."

"That's true, but the council is making an exception for Jonas because he's the new superintendent. Bob says he'll learn things there he needs to know."

For Bob to allow Jonas to witness the tribe's most sacred ceremony astounded Courtney. It confirmed that Jonas was now considered one of them.

"I won't be here. They'll have to find someone else."

"How do you know you won't be here? Charlie's the only one who knows the date, and he hasn't told the council yet. But it will be soon."

"I can't do it." Courtney shook her head adamantly.

"You'll have to. You're the only one from the tribe who can explain everything so Jonas will understand."

"Tell Bob I'm sorry, but I'm leaving in another week to visit my father before I go to Oklahoma."

"Bob won't like it." She turned and disappeared into the night, leaving Courtney more distraught than ever.

At four in the morning, Courtney was still wide awake. Even if she weren't going away, she couldn't possibly translate for Jonas. He'd never agree to it, anyway. Bob had no idea of the state of affairs between her and Jonas at this point.

Around five, Courtney gave up trying to sleep and took a shower, after which she cleaned her house from top to bottom. She needed physical activity to keep her from thinking, but nothing helped. She wished she were leaving for Zaire this minute. The way she was feeling, she'd never come back to Florida. Rosa was right about that.

By eight o'clock Courtney was ready to drive into Miami Beach and have breakfast with Linda, who was in the process of planning a farewell party for her. It was a lovely gesture but Courtney had never felt less like celebrating.

Bob Willie intercepted her as she started her truck. "Hi, Courtney."

She groaned when she heard his voice. "Hi, Bob."

"Rosa says you won't help at the Corn Dance."

"That's right. I'm leaving the state."

"The elders want you to translate."

"I know they do, but I can't."

"When do you leave?"

"A week from today."

"That's perfect. The ceremony will start day after tomorrow. You'll have time."

"I thought Charlie hadn't announced it yet."

"He told me early this morning."

"I still can't."

"I don't see the problem. You're just like your mother. You say no, but you mean yes."

"Don't ask me, Bob."

"You can't turn down the council once they've spoken their will. Besides, they said you can record the ceremony on tape."

Courtney's eyes widened in absolute astonishment. "Why would they allow such a thing?"

"Jonas explained that your work is important for the preservation of our culture, and I agree with him. Otherwise my grandchildren in the city might never know about our customs and rites. What do you say?"

What could she say? In granting her the opportunity to record the chants and songs of the Miccosukee's most sacred and ancient ceremony, they were bestowing complete trust in her. It was a compliment of the highest order, one that would please Courtney's mother if she were alive. It also revealed Jonas's powerful influence on the elders.

He knew how much it would mean to her to include the Corn Dance ritual in her thesis. Once again, she owed Jonas a debt of gratitude she could never repay.

"Does Jonas know I'll be translating?"

"Of course. He says you're the logical choice."

She rested her head against the back of the cab. "All right. I'll do it. Tell the elders I'm honored that they'd allow me this privilege."

"I'll tell 'em."

"Where will the ceremony take place?"

"Rosa'll show you."

They said goodbye and Courtney drove off in something of a daze. Although she could hardly bring herself to admit it, she was unbearably excited at the prospect of spending a little more time with Jonas before they went their separate ways.

Courtney's mother had allowed her to attend the Corn Dance when she was thirteen, but seeing it with Jonas at her side would be an entirely different experience. Especially as it lasted four days and nights. A wave of desire swept over her body at the mere thought of being with him again. Somehow she'd have to find a way to mask her feelings when they were together. After yesterday, however, it seemed obvious that Jonas would have no such problem.

As usual, he dominated her thoughts as she drove into the city. In fact, she was so preoccupied at breakfast, Linda commented on it. This, in turn, made Courtney feel terrible. Her best friend had gone to a great deal of trouble to plan a swimming party and barbecue for the coming weekend. Yet all Courtney could think about was Jonas and what it would be like when they saw each other again.

Asking her friend's forgiveness, Courtney tried to act enthusiastic, but Linda knew her too well and suggested they talk a little later in the week. Linda was still recovering from an unhappy love affair and could read the signs.

Courtney spent the rest of the day at the university finishing up last-minute business, then returned to the reservation to have dinner. Excitement was running high at Rosa's.

Tommie, the chief's son, planned to declare his intentions to the girl he wanted to marry at the Corn Dance. She lived along the Trail, and her parents expected her to be wooed and courted in the traditional way.

While Courtney ate her dinner and chatted with Tommie, Frank Bird came inside. She could tell he wanted to sit by her but didn't dare intrude since she was otherwise occupied. He finally left as Courtney continued to talk with Tommie, whose eyes were alight with happiness and hope. She envied him intensely for knowing what he wanted and being able to reach out for the girl he loved without any qualms.

Courtney returned to her place in a melancholy mood and slept poorly. To her surprise, Asiyaholo and another cousin were at her door early the next morning. They'd come for the Corn Dance but planned to do some hunting before the actual ceremony started. She fixed breakfast for them. Asiyaholo seemed pleased that Jonas would be attending the Corn Dance. He wanted to talk to him about fishing lures.

Later she discovered that most of the tribe members had gone to an undisclosed place near the Tamiami Trail to clean the dance grounds and repair the huts in preparation for the ceremony, which would start the next day.

Jonas hadn't made an appearance as yet, but she had no doubt that he'd be at the prescribed place at dawn. After their trip to the interior to visit her family, she'd learned enough about him to know he immersed himself totally in any endeavor he chose to undertake. And to know that he genuinely respected the tribe and their way of life.

As the June sky deepened to pink the next morning, Courtney showered and then put on her Miccosukee dress and moccasins. She wore no makeup, but could do nothing about her new hairstyle. Her one concession to vanity, however, was a dab of her favorite perfume. Jonas always noticed the little things, and she wanted his last memory of her to be a lingering one.

She knew without question that she'd never get over Jonas, not even if she lived to be as old as her grandmother. Courtney couldn't imagine being married to anyone else. That probably explained why she felt such fierce pleasure every time she thought of spending four days with him.

After breakfast, she and Rosa drove to the ceremonial site in Courtney's truck, which contained all her recording equipment.

"Jonas is waiting for you," Rosa said as they pulled up beneath a stand of slash pines.

Courtney noticed him immediately. He was dressed in jeans and a white knit sport shirt that clung to his chest and arms, revealing his hard strength. He appeared to be alone and in a pensive mood as his head turned at their approach.

As always, his striking looks and the magic of his presence haunted Courtney. She wondered whether she could make it through the next few minutes, let alone the next four days, without throwing herself at him.

"Courtney, Rosa." He nodded, and helped the older woman out of the truck before coming around to Courtney's side. But she'd already anticipated his intentions and jumped out to get her equipment from the back.

"I'll see you later," Rosa mumbled, walking off toward one of the huts in the distance. The women were busy preparing food while the men gathered to begin the ceremony.

Jonas helped her unload the equipment. His eyes glittered a strange jade-green in the early-morning light as he studied her features. She forced herself to look up into his unsmiling face.

"If it weren't for you, I'd never have been given this opportunity, Jonas. For what it's worth, I'm very grateful."

"Why are you thanking me? The tribe made the decision," he said tersely.

"Because you have a way of getting people to do what you want without their realizing it."

"And never count the cost," he finished bitterly.

"I didn't say that."

"I recall that you did."

"I—I've apologized for that," she whispered, feeling distinctly shaky. "If I'm going to translate for you, I'd like to pretend we're still friends."

"That's something we've never been—because you don't know the meaning of the word."

CHAPTER EIGHT

"BOB WILLIE KEEPS telling me I'm like my mother, and she was a loner. I suppose there's a lesson in there somewhere." She congratulated herself on keeping a steady voice because deep inside his accusation stung.

"Damn!" Jonas said, his body charged with emotion. "I shouldn't have said that, Courtney."

She rubbed a moist palm against her hip. "Why not? It's the truth. I jumped to all kinds of conclusions and made judgments about you based on what other people said and implied."

His eyes searched hers for an endless moment. "Just out of curiosity, who at the office led you to believe I'd use tribal funds to line my war chest?"

"I'd rather not say."

"Your loyalty to my father is nothing short of amazing."

"It wasn't your father," she shot back, not wanting to give Jonas any more reason to dislike Silas. He wasn't mollified.

"You seem to have developed a relationship with my father that none of the other office staff enjoyed. Why is that?"

She didn't understand what he was getting at but he sounded angry. "He often dictated late after everyone else went home. Since I was working the night shift, he would come into the computer room and talk to me. Through a casual comment, he found out about my interest in genealogy, and since that's his hobby, we struck up a friendship, I suppose."

"And being the kind of person you are, you listened and he started confiding in you, is that it?"

Her head reared back. "I wouldn't call it confiding, since he talked incessantly about you to everyone. Surely you're aware he worships the ground you walk on. He and my father are a great deal alike in that regard. Maybe it's the price we pay for being only children."

Jonas ran his hands through his black hair, still watching her closely. "Tell me about the Corn Dance."

The abrupt switch in the conversation surprised Courtney but she was glad to get off the topic of Jonas's father. "It's the Miccosukee's primary religious observance. The elders fast, the children are named, marriages are sanctioned and the tribal court convenes."

"What's happening now?" His gaze swerved to the grounds where the men and boys were piling wood.

"The medicine man is undergoing a ceremonial bath, then he'll direct all the activities. Later today there'll be a ball game, the women against the men."

"Can I join in?"

"Bob Willie expects you to. There'll be dancing tonight, and Tommie will offer for the girl he wants to marry."

"Only Tommie?"

"Any young man who wishes to marry can choose to dance with the maiden he prefers."

"And then what happens?"

She swallowed hard. "If she shows her pleasure by her laughter, or a certain light in her eye, or by her movements, he'll seek her out and talk to her. He might even ask her to eat at his fire. If things progress, they won't kiss, but he'll continue to court her. She'll eat the deer meat he's killed. And when both parents approve, a day will be appointed for them to marry."

"Where?"

"Well, on that special day she'll wait for him at her family's chickee. She'll be watching the trail anxiously, at sundown he'll arrive—if he's going to come." Her voice faded as she imagined herself waiting and waiting for Jonas, knowing in her heart that he'd never come for her. Not after what she'd done to him.

"And?" Jonas prompted. "Don't leave me hanging."

"She tells him she's happy he's there and he steps into the chickee. Then they begin their life together."

"No 'I do's'?"

"No." She shook her head. "It's a foregone conclusion, because they've already let each other know how they feel at the Corn Dance and word has reached the whole community.''

''If all marriages were transacted with such simplicity, most of the people in my profession would be out of a job,'' he said dryly. ''What if the woman changes her mind?''

''Then she doesn't welcome him into the chickee and he goes away.''

''He doesn't fight for her?''

''No. Each must come to the other of his or her own free will. The Miccosukee aren't violent.''

''Never?''

''Not to my knowledge.''

Jonas pursed his lips. ''Did your father participate in the Corn Dance?''

Every question he asked made her more uncomfortable. ''No. You're one of the few white men I've ever heard of who was actually invited to attend.''

She heard his sharp intake of breath. ''Then I suppose I ought to go over and start helping to gather wood.''

''Tonight they'll light a huge fire and perform several ceremonial dances before the courtship dance begins. I'll set up my equipment now, while you work with the men. When you're hungry, come and find me and we'll eat at one of the food chickees. Rosa's cooking pheasant and it's delicious.''

''I'll find you,'' he promised before walking away.

She couldn't take her eyes off him as he started toward the others. His confident masculinity, the way he carried himself, thrilled her. If only he still cared for her, as he once had. Then he would dance with her tonight. She would smile into his eyes and let him know by the swaying of her body that she wanted to live with him forever. She would sit by the fire with him, eat his food and nestle against him as the huge Florida moon rose in the sky.

One of the elders motioned to Courtney, bringing her back to reality. She followed him to the designated spot with her recording equipment and began to set things up. Once that was accomplished, she went over to the cooking chickee to help Rosa. Then, late in the afternoon, she took her place to record the evening's ceremonies.

The Dance of the Heron's Feather was as ancient as the tribe itself. While Courtney recorded the chant, Jonas watched the dancing with rapt concentration. The flames from the fire licked toward the velvet sky and cast flickering shadows on his dark skin as he sat cross-legged with the others in a semicircle of men.

Courtney's heart leaped in her breast every time she glanced in his direction. Tonight his eyes gleamed like emeralds. But throughout the rituals he hadn't looked at her once. Like the other men, he kept his attention riveted on the dancers. She might just as well have been invisible.

Wounded by his total indifference, she went back to the truck for another cassette to make sure she had a backup tape, in case anything happened while she was recording the Corn Dance.

She wasn't sure how long she could bear to watch the young lovers enact the mating ritual, knowing

Jonas was in the audience. She felt the night's enchantment; no longer did she try to conceal her love for him. If Jonas even glanced at her, he'd see desire and need in every flicker of her eyes, in every gesture of her body.

One by one the young men rose to their feet and each made his way to the woman of his choice. Courtney watched as the girl Tommie loved followed him into the dancing area and passed first in front of him, then behind him, never letting her eyes leave his as she swayed and pivoted to the chant.

Tommie stood proudly with his arms folded across his chest. He wasn't supposed to look at her. He was supposed to pretend that he didn't notice her, but Courtney saw his eyes rest on her from time to time with all the innocence and joy of young love. The scene moved Courtney almost to tears.

Then something happened that she should have been expecting. Frank Bird rose to his feet and started walking toward Courtney. Rosa had warned her about him but she hadn't taken the older woman seriously enough. What made it worse was that Courtney wasn't sitting with the other women and young girls. His intent expression filled her with dismay.

She knew that not dancing with him would offend him deeply. But if, out of politeness, she responded to his overtures, he would interpret it as courtship. Then she'd have to hurt him by telling him she couldn't accept his offer. This was a complication she'd never followed to its logical conclusion.

Her face must have clearly shown her panic and distress, because suddenly Jonas was on his feet and striding toward her. Since he was closer to Courtney than Frank was, he reached her first. The unexpected maneuver checked Frank's movements, and he spun around to find another girl in the crowd.

Courtney lifted her eyes to Jonas and detected a curious light in his. Her heart thudded. The blood pounded in her ears. It seemed Jonas was always coming to her rescue, but somehow, this time the gesture had assumed all the magic of the night.

Jonas had understood what was happening, and he'd prevented an awkward problem by intervening in the only acceptable way. But for Courtney it went much deeper than that. The Miccosukee part of her had taken over. In a trancelike move, she slowly rose to her feet and without any inhibitions whatsoever spoke to him with her eyes.

For the first time in their relationship she felt free to truly express her love, knowing that after the Corn Dance, she'd never see him again. Boldly she willed him to follow her into the circle with the other dancers. Some flicker of awareness leaped in his eyes as he acknowledged the challenge and moved with enticing male grace toward her.

She watched with fierce pride the way his strong arms folded across his broad chest and she wanted to shout to everyone assembled, ''He's my hunter, my warrior, my man—the father of my babies, my heart, my soul. He takes care of me, he's kind to me, he watches over me. He's the lover of my body. He's the healer of my mind.''

Like the lavender flowers that opened to the sun, revealing their purple throats, Courtney's love for Jonas poured forth as she made a pass in front of him, swishing her long skirt so it brushed sensuously against his trouser leg.

Everything and everyone else was forgotten as the chant became a living part of her. Pulse pounding, she gazed boldly into his shimmering eyes, willing him to know the secrets of her heart.

The ancient dance came to its climax and Courtney knelt before Jonas and lifted her hands, palms open, as if beseeching him to accept her gift. It said her heart was his for the keeping. She was giving it to him. Her message of love, like the scent of her perfume, was meant to rise in the hot night air to envelop and intoxicate the man who'd laid claim to her heart the first time their eyes met. Suddenly the chant stopped, but still Courtney's pulse surged. She got up from her knees to smile bewitchingly at Jonas before lowering her eyes like a bride.

Throughout the dance Jonas's face had remained impassive, the same as it was now. He followed the lead of the other young men and found an isolated spot around the fire. Courtney did as the other young women and walked behind him. When he was seated, she sat down next to him.

Unlike the others, however, she no longer sent him messages with her eyes. The dance had come to an end and she was weak from the ordeal. She felt as if she'd given up her soul, her very being, to him. Now she was an empty receptacle. Her moment for living was over, and all that was left was dust.

"I'll bring you some food," she said in a low voice and started to get up, not wanting to see the look of pity in his eyes.

"I'm not hungry," he answered unexpectedly, catching hold of her hand so she was forced to remain where she was.

The husky tone of his voice brought her back to reality in a hurry. "It's the custom, Jonas. Even if you don't want anything, I must get it for you."

She heard a deep sigh. "Make sure you come back, Courtney. You and I have some talking to do. If you take it into your head to run off tonight, be assured I'll come after you until I find you."

The restrained violence in his warning made her shiver and sent her hurrying toward one of the cooking chickees, where she could catch her breath for a minute. No one could have sounded less loverlike than Jonas did just now.

It was very possible that her dancing had embarrassed him. Now the whole tribe knew beyond question where her heart lay. She'd repaid his quick action in averting a crisis with Frank Bird by dancing a provocative dance that would have rivaled Salome's. *What had possessed her?*

Rosa's keen eyes stared straight into Courtney's as she dished up the pheasant and sweet potatoes, but thankfully the older woman said nothing. She didn't have to! Courtney's dancing had said it all.

Walking with as much dignity as she could manage, she carried their plates back to Jonas and placed them on the ground in front of him. As she started to sit down, she felt his eyes on her, following the line of her full curves, the contours of her face, the exotic shape of her dark brown eyes. A wave of heat suffused her tense body, almost suffocating her.

Jonas didn't touch his food. "That was quite a performance out there."

She tried to look everywhere except at him. "I did it for Frank."

"That's funny. I never noticed Frank, let alone anyone else after you started to dance." A pulse throbbed at his temple.

"I had to make it look convincing," she improvised. "With the eyes of all the tribe on him, it was important that he save face. Since you offered for me before he did, I let the tribe know you were my choice. That way, Frank wasn't offended. Now the tribe is saying it was meant to be, and no one's feelings are hurt. He chose someone else and can hold up his head because she returned his feelings."

His eyes narrowed. "But Frank wanted *you*."

"He only thought he wanted me. As I've told you before, I'm somewhat of a curiosity."

"You don't really believe that," Jonas drawled. "I've seen him watching you before. I saw the way he was looking at you tonight. If looks could kill, I'd be dead right now. So much for nonviolence."

"That's absurd."

Jonas reached for a piece of pheasant and bit into it with his beautiful white teeth. "You have no idea of your effect on a man, have you, Courtney?"

She had nothing to say to that and took a small taste of the sweet potatoes, but she could hardly swallow. "That was a daring move on your part tonight, Jonas, but I have to tell you I was more than a little relieved."

"Were you?"

Her eyes flashed. "Can you doubt it?"

"I don't know. There must be any number of men who want you to warm their chickees. What Frank did took a hell of a lot of courage. It isn't every man who would dare take you on, even if he was dying for the chance."

"Am I that unapproachable?" she asked in a dull voice.

"I'm the wrong person to answer that question." He began eating the sweet potatoes with apparent appetite. "So, what happens now?"

"What do you mean?" His question threw her.

"Is the ceremony over for tonight?"

"No. Now the men will retire to a designated spot and begin their fast. The women will sleep in the chickees. Tomorrow a drink will be prepared for the men to purge their spirits of all impurities. Then, there'll be more dancing. Later, some of the men will hunt for a white heron. The feathers will be used in another ceremony. The next day they'll hold court and mete out punishment. The thirteen-year-olds will be given names, and then everyone will eat the green corn, symbol of spring.''

Jonas appeared to be taking everything in. ''How many times have you attended this?''

''I saw it one other time as a child.''

He was pensive. ''What are all the new couples going to do at this point?''

''After they eat, they'll separate like the rest of the tribe.''

''And how will they get together again?''

''They'll find ways to meet over the next few days. Maybe they'll go for a walk in the woods or hide behind a bush and whisper to each other.''

''But they don't kiss?''

She fought to keep her voice steady. ''No. That's not their way.''

''What *is* their way?''

''I really don't know.'' Thoroughly flustered, she started to gather their plates.

''You mean to tell me you have no idea what went on between your father and your mother?''

She blushed. ''Yes, of course, but they were married.''

''So young couples in Miccosukee culture don't sleep with each other until their wedding night?''

''Not if they're traditionalists.''

''Is that what you are, Courtney?''

''I suppose I am. It's antiquated, I know.''

''Well, now I have answers to a few questions that have puzzled me from day one.'' Silence stretched between them.

Courtney looked around and discovered, to her surprise, that most of the couples had moved on. She'd been so absorbed with Jonas she'd forgotten where she was. "If you want to know what happens when the men get together for the fast, you'd better go with Bob Willie."

"Actually I'm going to join the police patrol the area tonight in case of some of those rowdies from outside the area should decide to cause trouble again. But I'll be back first thing in the morning."

His plan shouldn't have surprised her. As superintendent, his first responsibility was the safety and welfare of the people on the reservation. Even though the tribal police would be out in full force, Jonas would want to help. He took his responsibilities seriously; she knew that.

"I should get going, too. If you want more explanations in the morning, I'll be around setting things up for the medicine man's chant."

Jonas got to his feet and steadied her as she juggled their half-finished plates. "Will you be staying here all night with Rosa?"

"No. I'm going home to narrate what's already taken place. Then I'll make copies of the chants I've recorded."

"I hope you're not going back there alone."

"For heaven's sake, Jonas, I'm not a child."

"That's what has me worried. Get rid of those plates and I'll follow you to your place and take a look around to be sure you're safe."

She almost dropped the dishes. "You don't need to do that, and I don't want to take you away from your responsibilities." She turned quickly and almost ran toward the hut. She thrust the dishes at Rosa, who was gossiping with the other women as they cleaned up the chickee.

"Rosa? I'm going home, but I'll drive over here by seven tomorrow morning," she explained. She hurried off, not wishing to get into any kind of personal discussion with the older woman tonight.

When she finally left the ceremonial grounds with her tapes and recording equipment, Jonas was waiting in his truck, parked next to her pickup. He'd switched on his headlights to light the way for her as she climbed in and started her engine. Secretly, she was glad she didn't have to drive along the dirt track alone at this time of night.

Ten minutes later she was home and ready to wave Jonas off with a thank-you. But to her surprise he got out of his vehicle and followed her inside the house, checking the bedrooms and kitchen.

"What's wrong, Jonas? Why are you being so cautious?"

He rubbed the back of his neck thoughtfully. "With almost everyone attending the Corn Dance, you could be helpless if a bunch of inebriated hoodlums decided to pay the reservation a visit."

Until now she hadn't given that possibility a thought, but what he said made sense. There *had* been problems in the past few months; she'd heard about it from Rosa. "As you can see, no one's here. As soon as you leave I'll lock the door and make sure the windows are secure.''

His expression was grim. ''I don't like it. I think that under the circumstances I'd better stay awhile.''

Courtney set her things on the coffee table, then sank weakly onto the sofa. She hadn't expected to entertain him in her home again. In fact, nothing had gone as she'd imagined since she met Jonas at dawn. ''Are you expecting trouble tonight?''

''Bob and I discussed the possibility. I think I'll walk over to the clinic and the restaurant, then I'll come back. Don't open the door to anyone else.''

''I won't,'' she murmured, starting to feel frightened for him. She knew he could handle himself in any situation, but if a gang decided to attack him, he might need help. ''Be careful,'' she whispered.

''You sound as if you care,'' he mocked. ''I'll be back.'' He strode out and Courtney locked the door behind him. She realized she couldn't possibly get ready for bed until she'd seen him again safe and sound, so she went into the kitchen for a cola.

Then she sat at her computer for a while and tried to write her narrations. But she couldn't concentrate when Jonas might be returning any minute. Or worse, not returning—because he was dealing with an unpleasant and possibly dangerous situation.

After a half hour of pacing the living room floor, she began to panic and decided that the only thing she could do was to go outside and look for him. The idea of his being injured finally galvanized her into action.

Courtney had just slipped out the front door when Jonas suddenly appeared. "I thought I told you to stay put!"

"You were gone so long I got worried," she told him as he ushered her back into the house and slammed the door.

His green eyes held a trace of amusement. "And what did you think you'd accomplish if you found me lying in a heap in the dirt?"

She shuddered involuntarily. "I don't know. I didn't think that far."

He cocked his head. "That sounds a little out of character for you." The innuendo didn't escape Courtney.

"Would you like a drink?"

"No."

His mood had changed. She didn't know him like this. "Now that you're satisfied everything's all right here, are you going to go?"

"Are you asking me to leave?"

"Of course not."

"Good, because I have no intention of going."

She clung to the nearest chair. "Did you see anything suspicious outside?"

"No. But it's still early."

"Well, if there's nothing I can do for you—"

"I didn't say that," he murmured in a hoarse voice.

Her mouth went dry. "I think—"

But before she could get the words out he reached for her, cupping her face in his hands. Slowly, inexorably, his mouth lowered to hers and coherent thought ceased. There was only Jonas and the pressure of his mouth on hers. She'd wanted—needed—this for so long that she made no attempt to deny him. Jonas had ignited a fire and it was raging out of control.

Jonas crushed her body against him, molding every line and curve to his hard length. It was ecstasy. Courtney began to caress his chest and shoulders as she'd done a thousand times or more in her dreams, as she'd wanted to do earlier in the evening when she'd danced for him.

"Do you have any idea what you're doing to me?" he whispered against her throat where the scent of her perfume was sweetest. "I want you so much..."

Just being with Jonas aroused her desire for him, but tonight there was an intensity in his lovemaking that swept away all her inhibitions. "Love me, Jonas," she begged, covering his face with kisses, melting into him so he could feel the pounding of her heart.

Saying the words broke down the last barriers of reserve, as she wound her arms around his strong neck and caught his mouth to hers once more. "Stay with me tonight," she implored, curling her fingers in his black hair. He trembled at her touch, making her aware of her femininity and the strange power she had over him.

"Do you know what you're saying?" His deep voice resounded through her, as his mouth caressed her eyes, her mouth, her hair, placing kisses that made her blood flow like dark wine through her veins.

"All I know is how I feel right now," she confessed. "Because I'm with you. I've wanted this for so long." Her voice shook with emotion. She kissed the hand cradling her cheek, as though she couldn't get enough of him.

"What if I make you pregnant?" he murmured against her throat before sliding his hands over her upper arms and holding her apart from him. "There might be consequences."

The meaning of his words took forever to reach her consciousness, but when it did, a cold chill invaded her body and she eased herself out of his arms while she still could. She ought to be thanking him for keeping his head while she'd spun totally out of control. But all she felt was mortification and a kind of sickness, because he'd been the one to call a halt to their lovemaking.

He'd left the ultimate decision up to her, but it was the decision he wanted. She was sure of that. He might still desire her, but something had died. Something intangible had crept in to change Jonas. They could never go back to the way things had once been.

"Courtney?" He still held her, searching her face relentlessly as if he were looking for something he couldn't find. A bleakness entered his eyes as she moved out of his arms completely.

Forcing a smile, she said, "It wouldn't be a good idea to risk getting pregnant just before I leave for Oklahoma. You're right. I didn't realize what I was saying or doing just now. It must be the effects of the dance or something else equally foolish."

He said her name again, a harsh whisper this time, but she was no longer the love-crazed woman who'd offered herself so blatantly, without any thought but to belong to him for one night.

"You know," she began in a tremulous voice, "it's embarrassing how many times I've had to thank you. But rest assured you can walk out that door tonight and know your days of rescuing me are over."

"What are you talking about?" he asked angrily. He took a step toward her and she backed away.

"I'd like you to leave. If you need a translator tomorrow, Rosa will be only too glad to help. She's one of your greatest fans."

Jonas's face looked gray in the dim light of the table lamp. "You know you don't want me to go, Courtney. I only brought up the possibility of your becoming pregnant out of concern for you."

"You've done your good deed for the night. Please go."

A grimace marred his features. "If there's trouble, no one will be around to help you."

"You're not my keeper, Jonas."

"You've made that abundantly clear for some time now." The air was heavy with tension. "I think you've finally convinced me." He was out her front door in an instant.

If Courtney believed that her pain couldn't get any worse, she was wrong. Without conscious thought she sat down in the nearest chair, unable to move until she heard the first twitter of birds signalling the break of dawn. Only then did her body release the pain that held it prisoner and she began to cry, great heaving sobs that lasted so long she didn't emerge from her house to go to the ceremonial grounds till afternoon.

Her eyes puffy, she searched for Jonas among the men playing ball, but didn't see him anywhere. Automatically her gaze went to the area of the cooking chickees, where she caught sight of Rosa preparing meat.

"What happened to you?" Rosa's blunt speaking was the last thing Courtney needed right now.

"Did you translate for Jonas this morning?" Courtney asked, choosing to ignore Rosa's probing question.

"No. I thought you did."

Fear ripped through her heart. "Have you seen him at all?"

"No. You two mad at each other again?"

"Rosa," Courtney cried out in exasperation, "I have to know if anyone's seen him on the grounds. When he left last night he was going out on patrol, but should have returned because I know he wanted to watch Charlie dance."

"Jonas can take care of himself."

"I know, but I'd still feel better if I knew he'd been seen by someone. Could you get word to Bob Willie?"

The older woman didn't say anything for a minute. "I'll see what I can do. You finish roasting the meat while I talk to the chief." Courtney realized that although Rosa would never admit it, she was concerned, too.

The delicious smells coming from the chickee permeated the atmosphere but Courtney had no appetite as she tried to identify Jonas's dark hair and lean body among the various groups of men assembled.

The second Courtney saw Rosa's solemn face, she ran to meet her. "What did you find out?"

"Jonas won't be attending the rest of the Corn Dance ceremony."

"Why? What happened?" she cried out in alarm.

"He got word to Bob Willie that his father's had a heart attack."

"Oh, no!" Poor Jonas. For this to happen so soon after he'd left the firm, particularly with the two of them estranged, was the worst kind of news. Courtney could just imagine how Jonas would blame himself.

After last night's episode, Jonas wouldn't appreciate her inquiring after his father, or offering sympathy. She didn't dare compound their problems by trying to reach him. He'd resent her intrusion in his personal life and probably ignore any messages she left for him.

But she could call the firm and make inquiries.

"Rosa, I have to go to Miami. I'm not sure when I'll be back. If I showed you how to work my equipment, would you record tonight's chants and watch over my things until I return?"

"I'll do it. You go to Jonas. He needs you now." For once Rosa sounded totally approving, which showed just how much the older woman cared for

Jonas. It also revealed her complete ignorance of the true state of affairs between him and Courtney.

Even if Courtney were to tell Rosa everything, the older woman would scoff and tell her she was just being headstrong like her mother. Rosa had witnessed Courtney's performance at the dance, and no power on earth would convince her it wasn't the real thing. That was the trouble. In Courtney's heart it *was* real and nothing she could say or do would ever change that.

CHAPTER NINE

"COURTNEY? I know you're tired, but I haven't had a chance to thank you properly for all those plant samples you collected. They're fantastic!"

Linda's party was over and everyone else had left. Courtney had put on the performance of her life in front of their friends, but she couldn't keep up the pretense any longer. She wished Bryce Towers would leave.

"I hope I brought back something that intrigued you."

He was the typical professor, with his trim beard, mustache and dark-framed glasses. "You brought several species I haven't found anywhere else. The next time you go to the interior, can I tag along?"

Courtney smiled. "When I'm planning my next trip, I'll give you a call, but I don't think I'll be visiting my family for another year."

"I heard you got your grant. Congratulations! You're going to be famous while I'm still struggling to get work out of my undergraduates."

"You don't get famous in our profession, Bryce. You just get old and frustrated."

He eyed her soberly. "Well, you got the frustrated right, anyway. I don't suppose you'd go out to dinner with me before you leave Miami."

"I can't," she was able to answer honestly. "I'm flying to Zaire in the morning to visit my father, and from there I'm booked straight through to Oklahoma. Otherwise I'd love to."

"Sorry, Bryce." Linda broke in on their conversation, "Someone wants Courtney on the phone." Courtney's heart knocked in her breast. It might be Jonas. But Linda's almost imperceptible shake of her head indicated that she didn't know who it was.

"Excuse me, Bryce," Courtney said as calmly as she could, wondering who would be phoning now. She decided to take the call in the bedroom she'd been sharing with Linda for the past two nights. She sat down on one of the twin beds and reached for the receiver. "Hello?"

"Is this Courtney Blake?" The voice was a woman's, and familiar.

"Yes," she said slowly, and suddenly she knew who it was. "Mrs. Payne?"

"Yes. Sylvia from the office told me I could reach you at this number. If this is a bad time, I can call back."

"It's fine. How are you? How's Mr. Payne? I'm so sorry about his heart attack. I hope he's all right."

"It was very minor, Courtney, and he's already home from the hospital. Provided he minds the doctor, he should live a long, full life. He wants you to know he received the flowers. They're beautiful. We all appreciate them."

"I'm glad I could let him know in some way that I care. He was a wonderful man to work for."

"He sings your praises as well, my dear. Is it true you're leaving Florida to do research elsewhere?"

"Yes. In Oklahoma."

"Jonas mentioned something to that effect a few weeks ago. How long will you be away?"

"At least eighteen months, maybe longer."

There was a long silence. "I had no idea you'd be gone so long. Perhaps before you go we could have you over to the house for dinner. Would that be possible?"

"As lovely as that sounds, I'm afraid it isn't." She could hardly talk for the emotion. "I'm leaving for Zaire in the morning and I won't be coming back here."

"Zaire? Your father lives there, doesn't he? How nice that you'll get to see him before you start another project."

"Yes. I'm looking forward to it."

"I'm sure you are, but I have to tell you I'm sorry I didn't know about this sooner. Silas will be disappointed, too. We both enjoyed your company when Jonas brought you to the house."

Courtney didn't think she could handle their conversation much longer. Talking to Jonas's mother brought him back too forcefully. And something about Mrs. Payne's comments led Courtney to believe Jonas had told his mother very little about their problems.

"I enjoyed getting to know you, too. Please give my best to Mr. Payne."

"Of course I will. Is Jonas taking you to the airport?"

The unexpected question made Courtney catch her breath. "Actually my best friend, Linda, is going to drive me. Jonas is on call day and night in his new position as superintendent so he won't be available," she improvised.

There was another distinct pause. "He loves that job. Much to Silas's disappointment, I think Jonas has found his life's work. Who would ever have dreamed it?"

"I'm not sure I understand," Courtney murmured, curious to know what she had to say.

"I don't think I did at first either," she said with a chuckle. "When Jonas told his father he wanted to leave the firm to become a superintendent, Silas thought he was kidding. The next thing we knew, he had his appointment."

Taking a deep breath, Courtney said, "Then you think this is a permanent move for Jonas?"

"Definitely."

"I thought there might be a chance he'd go into politics."

"Heavens, no! Oh, maybe years ago Jonas entertained the idea because his father pushed for it. But later on he became intrigued with Indian law and I don't think he ever gave politics another thought."

As if in a trance, Courtney slid off the bed, trying to check the flow of adrenaline surging through her body. "But Mr. Payne always talked about it."

"I know." She laughed goodnaturedly. "He's always been involved in politics and hoped Jonas would get caught up in it, too. But things didn't turn out that way. Since his heart attack, I think he's finally realized Jonas has to be his own person.

"And if I know my son, he'll probably be buried in reservation business for the rest of his life, and we'll be lucky if we get to see him on holidays. I'm sure you've seen much more of him than we have."

Anything else Mrs. Payne said, Courtney didn't hear. The receiver had slipped from her hand and fallen to the floor. Feeling ill, she groped for it and put it back to her ear, but her heart was pounding so hard she couldn't think, let alone listen.

"I didn't mean to go on about Jonas. I've kept you when you're trying to get ready to leave. Please don't forget us. The next time you come to Miami, give us a call. We'd love to see you again."

"Thank you, Mrs. Payne." Courtney could hardly get the words out. "I'll do that. Goodbye."

"Courtney?" Linda's voice rang out. "Can you come and say goodbye to Bryce?" Linda walked into the bedroom but came to an abrupt halt. "Courtney?" she cried in alarm. "You look like you've seen a ghost. What's wrong?"

"I can't face Bryce right now. Tell him anything."

Anxiety deepened Linda's blue eyes. "This had to do with Jonas. Has something happened to him? Tell me!"

"Oh, Linda." Courtney shook her head in anguish. "I've done the unforgivable."

"Wait right there while I get rid of Bryce." Linda was back within minutes, but Courtney didn't feel she could burden her friend anymore then she already had.

"I'm all right. I think the best thing for me would be to help you clean up the house. I'll start washing the dishes and you can dry."

"Wait a minute!" Linda stood her ground. "If you think I'm going to let the guest of honor work at her farewell party, then you can think again."

"Please, Linda," Courtney begged. "If I don't keep busy I'll go mad."

They shared a long, silent look, full of understanding. Linda sighed. "When you want to talk, let me know." By tacit agreement they went into the living room to gather up the glasses and plates.

The rest of the night passed in a blur. Courtney had already put her truck in storage, along with her furniture; she'd send for everything after settling in Oklahoma.

The next morning, there was nothing left to do but put her suitcases in the trunk of Linda's car and leave for the airport. It was during the drive that she finally broke down and told Linda everything.

"Do you want to know what I think?" Linda eyed her soberly while they waited at a light. "I think you ought to put your plans on hold and go after Jonas."

Courtney shook her head vehemently. "You don't know him like I do, Linda. He'll never forgive me for what I did to him, for what I believed about him. It's over." She shivered.

"I don't think so," Linda insisted stubbornly.

"I know so."

"But hasn't that been the trouble all along?" she asked, glancing at Courtney, eyebrows raised. "You always assume something, yet Jonas has proved you wrong every time. I think you're afraid."

Courtney squirmed uncomfortably. "In what way?"

"I think what happened to your parents had a devastating effect on you without your realizing it. Deep down you believe that you'll end up alone like your mother because you're convinced you and Jonas won't be able to make it any more than your parents did."

Courtney stared out the window without seeing anything. "You're right, Linda. I'm terrified."

"But just think how much more terrifying it would be if you went through your whole life without Jonas and then you found out it didn't have to be like that, and the only obstacle that stood in the way was your own fear and pride."

"My mother had too much pride. Bob Willie says I'm just like her. He says she was paranoid, and I am, too."

"You are. But you've got to remember that your mother was still a courageous woman. She reached out for what she wanted even though it went against everything in her culture. You're not faced with the same odds. Think about that."

Courtney *was* thinking. It was all she'd been doing since talking to Jonas's mother. "I don't honestly know where I'd be today without your friendship, Linda. And I'll think about what you've said while I'm at Dad's."

"That's good. And when you've come to some conclusions, call me."

"I'll do that anyway."

ORIGINALLY Courtney had planned to stay at her father's for three weeks, but ten days into the visit, she booked a flight back to Miami. After confiding in her father, who encouraged her to take Linda's advice, Courtney felt she had to see Jonas one more time. As her father said, Jonas might refuse to see her or talk to her, but if she didn't take the risk, she'd never know for sure.

The minute she left the airport, she took a taxi to Jonas's house. Despite her exhaustion from the long flight, she was afraid her courage would desert her if she didn't go to him immediately. Since it was a Sunday morning, she thought she might surprise him at his house, but she had no idea of his routine or how he spent his free time since he'd become the superintendent at Red Mangrove.

She paid the driver and hurried up the steps to ring the bell. The morning heat was sweltering and she removed the jacket of a new lemon-yellow sundress she'd changed into at the airport.

Delia opened the door and greeted Courtney with warm affection, once she got over her surprise. In the next breath she told her that Jonas wasn't home.

"Do you know where he might be today?"

"At the reservation. He might as well live there now."

"On Sunday?" she asked incredulously.

"It doesn't make any difference to him, Courtney. Since he's started to work out there, he rarely comes home except to read his mail or change his clothes."

Courtney ran a slender hand through her hair. "I was hoping to see him today."

"You're welcome to come inside and use the phone. His secretary might know where he is. You could call her at home, or try calling the reservation."

"That would be wonderful."

"Go right into Jonas's study. You'll find all the numbers you need on his desk. While you're doing that, I'll fix you some fresh lemonade."

Courtney thanked the housekeeper and made her way to Jonas's private office. The room contained a library worth a fortune, its style, from the gleaming polished floors and beautiful rugs, to the classic marble fireplace, revealed a simplicity and strength reminiscent of the man himself.

But there was one significant change since the last time she'd been here. A new painting hung over the fireplace, a painting that dominated the room. She stared at it for endless moments. It was like looking in a mirror at her own reflection, and yet it wasn't. She didn't recognize this Courtney. A small bronze plaque at the bottom of the frame held the inscription, *Princess Suklatiki of the Glades*.

Her eyes misted over. Jonas had commissioned someone to paint the picture of her from the photograph he'd taken during their canoe trip.

Was the love light in her eyes part of the artists' creation, or had her feelings for Jonas always been that transparent?

The woman in the painting looked enchanted. The dappling sunlight on the water, on her waist-length chestnut hair, and skin, on her Miccosukee dress, caused the painting to literally shimmer with refracted light. The effect was breathtaking.

"It's a shame you cut your hair, but luckily it'll grow back." Delia chatted amicably as she brought Courtney a drink and stood to admire the picture with her. "Jonas loves that painting. I guess you hadn't seen it before."

"No," was all she could say because of the enormous lump in her throat. Out of courtesy, she sipped the lemonade, but all the while her thoughts were racing ahead. "Delia, if Jonas is still on the reservation, I'll find him. Thank you for everything. I'll just call a cab and go."

Within a few minutes, a taxi had pulled up in front of the house.

"What shall I tell Jonas if he calls or comes home?"

Courtney was already breathless with excitement. "Don't tell him anything. Let me surprise him."

"He'll be surprised all right. Aren't you supposed to be in Zaire?"

"Yes," she said over her shoulder before climbing into the backseat of the taxi.

By noon Courtney had got her truck as well as a few essential articles out of storage and was headed west on the Tamiami Trail toward Red Mangrove.

Rosa looked up as Courtney entered the restaurant later that afternoon. "It's about time you came back. What took you so long?"

Courtney grinned at her mother's best friend. "I'm my mother's daughter, remember? Everyone said she was pigheaded. I guess I inherited her most memorable trait."

"Well, I guess that isn't so bad. When your hair's back to normal, I don't suppose anyone will remember."

Courtney started to laugh; she couldn't help it. But her laughter subsided when Rosa said bluntly, "He's not here."

There was no need to ask whom she was talking about. "Do you know where he is?"

"No, but I imagine Bob Willie does."

"Do you know where Bob is?"

"I might. The trouble is, Bob Willie's not that happy with you right now."

"Since when is that anything new?"

"He says you're always causing trouble for Jonas."

"Do you agree?" Courtney couldn't refrain from asking.

"Are you going to cause more trouble?"

"What do you think?" She stared the older woman down. "Will you act as my mother and announce my wedding to Bob?"

A rare smile illuminated Rosa's face. "I think I'll have to talk with the chief. You go in the back room and lie down for a while. Didn't you just fly halfway around the world?"

"Yes."

"How's your father?"

"He's wonderful."

"Have some pumpkin bread. It's fresh from the oven."

"I thought you'd never offer."

"Humph!"

Courtney didn't know if Rosa purposely let her sleep the rest of the day, or if she didn't have any news to give her until evening. All Courtney knew was that she awakened a little after seven, feeling disoriented from the time change.

Rosa stood in the doorway. "Good. You're awake."

Courtney scrambled to her feet, suddenly wide-awake. "Did you talk to Bob or couldn't you find him?"

"I found him. Jonas has gone fishing."

"Where?"

"He didn't say."

"Did you tell Bob about the marriage?"

"I didn't have to. Charlie saw you drive in and told him." Somehow Charlie knew everything.

"Rosa," Courtney said in a subdued voice, "this is serious. I have to find Jonas and talk to him. Didn't Bob give you a clue?"

"Nope. He said Jonas took a few days off and went fishing."

"Do you believe Bob?"

"Don't you?"

After a sustained pause Courtney admitted that she did. "In the morning I'm going to try to find him."

"Asiyaholo brought your canoe back. It's out in the shed. You stay here tonight."

"Thank you, Rosa. I can see why Mother considered you her best friend." On that note Courtney hurried out to get her canoe. She wanted to place it at the put-in point and pack her gear before dark.

Experiencing a sense of déjà vu, Courtney paddled away from shore the next morning as the sun appeared above the horizon. It was one of those cloudless skies, and the heat would be intense long before noon.

Jonas could be anywhere, of course, but her instincts told her he'd find a spot near a deserted chickee somewhere in the preserve where he could camp for the night and prepare a meal. If he wanted to be totally alone, he probably wouldn't fish where he'd caught the bass, because it was too close to her family's hummock. She also doubted he'd camp by the lagoon, because of the alligators.

There was one other place she could think of, a small, secluded haven that would provide him with all the fish he could catch. They'd passed it on their way to her grandmother's. She struck out for that spot, figuring she'd reach it some time after lunch.

The Glades were alive with exotic flowers that had only been tiny buds when Jonas had followed her here before. For once she didn't mind the stifling heat. Her whole mind and heart were concentrated on him. She refused to consider the possibility that she might not find him.

When she was in the vicinity of the great white herons' rookery, she made a detour off the main waterway and traveled through the vegetation so she'd reach the back of the hummock without being observed. That way, Jonas wouldn't know of her presence before she was ready to reveal herself.

The canoe slid noiselessly into the saw grass outcropping and Courtney jumped out to secure it. In her moccasins she could move about as stealthily as the animals inhabiting the hummock.

Quickly she set off through the forest, with its profusion of colors and scents. It was like stepping into a primeval world, full of giant mahogany trees, overhead air plants and Spanish moss. Courtney particularly loved the resurrection ferns that formed small forests of their own on the limbs of the larger trees. She took a deep breath; the air felt steamy and motionless. Had Jonas come here, or was it only her own desperate hope that had convinced her?

The minute she saw a tarp hanging from the roof of the exposed west side of the chickee, Courtney knew she'd found him. She cocked her head and listened for his movements, but all she could hear was the noisy chatter of birdsong and the buzzing of insects.

She imagined he was out fishing by a promising hole, and crept closer, scanning the shorelines for signs of his kayak. To her relief it wasn't there. Without wasting another second, she hurried back to her canoe and began carrying her gear to the lookout spot behind the chickee. He might not return for hours, but she wasn't taking any chances. The important thing was to be ready for him by sundown.

The day literally dragged by until she was sick with nervous excitement. Jonas was too expert a woodsman not to return to camp at a decent hour. It was the unwritten law of the Glades.

As she rested her head against her pack, she heard the dip of his paddle and lunged forward on her knees to watch him through the leaves.

He wore white shorts and thongs. His magnificent bronzed body had a sheen that emphasized his lean physique. He jumped out of his kayak into the water, and for a moment disappeared beneath the surface. Then he walked onto the shore with his black hair attractively disarrayed and dripping.

He pulled a catch of fish from his kayak and started toward the chickee. Courtney fastened her gaze on his face, caressing every strong line and angle of his features. His eyes took on the exact hue of the greenery. Their beauty made her gasp softly and she wanted to announce herself immediately. But the time wasn't right.

She watched him spray on repellent, then slip into a white T-shirt. He cleaned his catch, and soon she could smell the delicious odor of the fish sizzling in the frying pan.

He fixed himself a plate and started to eat. Instead of sitting down on a camp stool he'd brought, he leaned against one of the poles and stared out across the shoreline as if deep in thought. His food didn't appear to interest him very much.

Courtney looked up at the sky. The sun was ready to drop below the horizon. Now was the time to make her move. With her heart knocking against her ribs she worked her way through the dense vegetation, picking up her long skirt so it wouldn't catch against the prickles.

She made a wide circle so that when she came into view, it would seem as though she'd arrived from the water where he'd put his kayak. Close to fainting from fear and uncertainty, she stepped into the clearing.

CHAPTER TEN

"DEAR LORD," she heard him whisper as she approached, coming to a halt only a few yards away. The color had all but drained from his face. Never in her life had she seen Jonas look so shocked, and if her sight didn't deceive her, so vulnerable.

His hands still held the plastic plate and fork. He didn't move from his position on the chickee platform. It was as if he'd been frozen in mid-action.

"I didn't mean to startle you," she said softly.

Perhaps it was hearing her voice that provoked movement, because he tossed his plate and fork on the camp table and stood defiantly with his hands on his hips.

"You don't mean to do a lot of things," he finally responded with a hostility that wounded her. "I'm not going to ask why you've suddenly shown up here, of all places. Give me ten minutes and I'll be gone."

"Jonas—" she cried out. "I came to find you."

His face closed up. "I can't imagine why, and so help me I don't want to know. If I haven't made myself clear, then I'll spell it out. I want to be left alone."

In a bold move she stepped closer so she could see the pulse throbbing at his temple. "I know." She swallowed hard. "But I have to talk to you."

His bark of laughter sounded cruel. "That's too bad, isn't it? I recall a time when I needed to talk to you, but you conveniently left town. That's what I'm going to do now."

He turned his back on her and started to make preparations to leave the chickee. She couldn't let him go.

"I'm in love with you," she confessed.

He spun around with a duffel bag in hand. "Give it up, Courtney. You're the one person I know who doesn't even understand the word, let alone know how to give it."

If she hadn't seen the painting over his fireplace, she would have left by now, utterly devastated by his rejection, but feminine instincts older than time kept her standing exactly where she was.

With great daring she said, "Is that why you keep a picture of me in the study?"

His head reared back. Her question was obviously the last thing he expected. "How do you know about that?"

"I went to your house directly from the airport yesterday morning, hoping to talk to you. Delia let me in to your study to make a phone call, and that's when I saw it."

His hand curled into a fist around the drawstring of his bag. "What do you want, Courtney?" The ferocity in his voice shocked her.

"I want you." Her declaration hovered in the steamy air between them like a live wire. When he didn't respond, she moved closer. "The sun's going down, Jonas."

"What the hell am I supposed to do about that? I'll be out of here in a minute, then you can have the place to yourself!" He was recklessly throwing the rest of his stores in the other duffel bag.

She'd never seen Jonas like this before. Always in the past, he'd been the one in total control. His agitated behavior gave her the courage to follow through with her plan even though her legs were shaking.

"Don't tell me you've forgotten the Corn Dance already," she chided gently.

"What are you talking about?" He practically ripped the tarp from the rafters.

"Sundown is a time of great significance in Miccosukee culture. Don't you remember?"

"I'm sure you'll refresh my memory." His rudeness would have been daunting if she hadn't picked up on certain signals that told her he was on the verge of erupting.

"Sundown is the time when the man comes to the chickee of his beloved to mate forever."

His face was a frozen pale mask. "I don't see the connection." He knelt on the floor of the chickee and started to roll up his sleeping bag.

"In matters of the heart, a Miccosukee woman can break tradition and seek out her beloved. You danced with me at the ceremony. It's now my right to approach your chickee. I've come for you, Jonas."

He paused in his exertions and darted her an unfathomable glance. "Would you mind repeating that?"

She took a deep breath, staring into his angry eyes. "You chose me at the spring ritual, and I danced for you. Tonight is the appointed time for our marriage. The tribal elders have been informed. I've walked the trail to your hut. I'm waiting for you to tell me you're happy I've come."

Something flickered in his eyes and he went perfectly still. "You told me you were dancing for Frank Bird."

"That was because I was too afraid to tell you the truth."

"What truth is that?" he demanded fiercely, yanking the knot of his sleeping bag.

Her eyes glistened. "That I've loved you from the first moment I saw you. That the night of the Corn Dance, my heart was so filled with love for you, I had to let you know how I felt, or die a little."

His features tightened so they looked like the relief on a coin. "You told me to leave your house that night."

"I begged you to stay with me that night," she corrected him. "It was you who backed off."

"And you know why!" he lashed out.

"There was a time when you wouldn't have been concerned if a baby had resulted."

He rose slowly to his feet. "There was a time when I thought it a foregone conclusion you'd be my wife!

I would have been overjoyed if I'd made you pregnant."

Courtney's breasts heaved. "Maybe now you understand why it hurt so terribly when you stopped our lovemaking to remind me of the consequences. I wanted to lie in your arms all night long and show you how much I loved you. I wanted your baby more than anything in the world!"

"When did this miraculous change of heart suddenly take place?" The sarcasm spilled out of him.

"Don't you know I was praying you'd ask me to marry you before you left for Washington?" she asked in trembling voice. "But you didn't."

"Because I was planning to propose to you when you came to Washington. My appointment was going to be a sort of wedding gift for you."

"Jonas—" she cried softly. "How could I possibly have known that? And then, when your father said you were going to run for governor soon, and that you'd be marrying Laura, I went into shock. It all seemed so definite."

"My father's always been too caught up in my life, too ambitious for me. But when he made that announcement, he went too far."

"Maybe now you can understand why it was so easy for me to believe what I overheard Raynor telling Laura—that you'd taken advantage of the tribe to raise money for your campaign. Laura didn't deny it. Then my name was brought into the conversation. She told Raynor I was never a threat. She also said you were hoping I'd be gone from the firm before you returned from Washington."

Jonas swore violently. "Laura is the daughter of my father's best friend, who died years ago. My father took it on himself to watch out for her and help shape her career. Somewhere along the line they both decided she'd make the perfect wife for me. You could say that was the start of our estrangement."

Courtney believed him. She moved closer. "I know now it was all a lie. I'd begun to realize that, and talking to your mother simply confirmed it."

"You talked to Mother?" He was clearly surprised. "When?"

Courtney shifted her weight, aware of night falling all around them. For the first time, she could tell, he was really listening. "About two weeks ago. I phoned the law firm to ask about your father and left Linda's phone number with Sylvia, the receptionist. I asked her to keep me posted on his condition. Sylvia must have given your mother the number because she called me at Linda's to thank me for the flowers I sent him."

Jonas rubbed the back of his neck. "They meant a great deal to Father. Especially since he's been feeling a certain remorse for what he said and did in your hearing, Courtney. He never meant to hurt you. But his ambition for me blinded him to reality. This heart attack has made him take a second look. I never thought I'd see the day that would happen."

"I'm glad," she whispered, thankful Jonas and his father had reconciled. "Your mother said much th same thing to me. She also made it clear you'd be interested in Indian affairs since law school and had found your life's work. Can you ever forgive me for doubting you?''

There was a lengthy pause. "I can see now that waiting until I received my appointment before asking you to marry me was exactly the wrong thing to do, because it left you so vulnerable. But I wanted everything to be in my favor so you wouldn't have any reservations about becoming my wife."

"Reservations?" Courtney was incredulous. "I wanted to marry you under any circumstances. If anything, I was afraid there was something lacking in *me* that kept you from proposing. I found myself looking for reasons why marriage to you couldn't or wouldn't work. My parents divorce, for instance. They loved each other so much, but Daddy said Mother's fear of failure separated them in the end."

"You're not your mother, Courtney. Our situation isn't comparable."

"Linda said the same thing."

"Linda's a discerning woman. But the only thing that matters is that *you* believe it."

"I—I wouldn't have come for you if there'd been the slightest doubt in my mind."

A strange, almost painful tension hovered between them. Jonas looked around him, as if aware of his surroundings for the first time. "Where's your canoe?"

"Behind the hummock," she answered, her heart in throat.

His eyes played over her face for endless moments. "And your gear?"

"In the woods behind the chickee."

He sucked in his breath. "I'll worry about your things another day, maybe in a month, because I think it'll take that long before I'll feel like doing anything but making love to you." His voice resonated to her inner core. "Is there a magic word I should use to invite you to cross my threshold?"

"Jonas," she half sobbed as she covered the distance between them, her feet barely touching the ground. She literally threw herself into his arms and clung to him.

"Darling," he cried softly, burying his face in her hair, sweeping her off the ground to crush her to him. "My wife, my love."

His mouth roamed feverishly over her face, pressing kisses against each exquisite feature. "My beautiful Suklatiki. I thought we'd really lost each other. I came out here to be alone and try to reconcile myself to a future without you. I believed you were gone for good.

"But the Glades are full of you. Everywhere I look, everything I see, touch and smell reminds me of you." His voice trembled. "Don't ever leave me again, Courtney. I couldn't take it."

"Neither could I." She searched for his mouth and moaned in ecstasy as his kiss brought her alive. "Forgive me for hurting you," she whispered when she could draw breath. "I'll never knowingly hurt you again."

"Darling—" he caressed her lips sensuously "—before this honeymoon begins in earnest, we have to talk about your grant."

"I don't have to accept it, Jonas."

His hands stilled in her hair. "Yes, you do. I know it's tied up with your commitment to your mother never to forget your heritage. And there's a teaching position at the university waiting for you when it's completed."

"Jonas, I can't leave you for eighteen months. Not now."

"We'll work it out and take turns flying back and forth to be with each other on the weekends. It'll be like a honeymoon every time we're together."

Courtney's heart filled to overflowing. "You'd be willing to do that for me?"

His answer was to enfold her tightly in his arms. "I fell in love with an anthropologist. Eighteen months will pass soon enough and then we'll always be together. How does it sound if we divide our time between here and the house in Miami Beach?"

"Heavenly. But—"

"But what?" he asked immediately.

"What if I get pregnant?" she whispered against his questing mouth.

Jonas responded with a chuckle. "There are ways around that, my darling."

"But I want to have your baby," she insisted, pressing her face against his neck.

"I want that, too," he murmured into her hair, "but we can wait nine more months before getting started on it."

She pulled out of his arms. "Does that mean you want to put off our marriage till then? Is that why you haven't made love to me yet?"

The deep laughter rumbled out of him. "Why, Mrs. Payne. You're shameless."

"Stop teasing me, Jonas. I'm aching to love you."

"And you think I'm not?" he demanded, his voice charged with emotion. "Let's get something straight at the outset. I want to make absolutely certain we understand each other before I start loving you, because when that happens, the time for talking will long be over."

When she didn't say anything he drew her back into his arms and gave her a long, lingering kiss. "You have nothing more to say? To ask?"

"Nothing!"

His breath caught. "Then you've just said the magic word, Mrs. Payne." His voice was sensuous as he put her gently away from him.

"What are you doing?"

"I'm going to light the lantern."

"Why?" she whispered.

"Because I want to look at you."

The light it gave off was strong enough to reveal the blush on her cheeks.

"Your eyes are shining exactly as they did the night you danced for me. Dance for me again, Courtney, only this time I want to see the beauty of your body without any other adornment. Certain traditions among your mother's people are still foreign to me, but your rites of love appeal to my deepest emotions. Show me again that I'm your warrior, your hero.'' His green eyes shimmered. ''I'll try to be all those things to you forever. I swear it.''

With trembling hands she started to undo her dress. ''I'll be your comfort, your haven. I'll give you rest. I'll provide your pleasure forever. I swear it.''

His chest rose and fell. ''Every spring I'll bring you here to renew our vows.''

A mysterious smile illuminated her face. ''Every spring I'll dance for you. Only for you.'' Her voice trailed off. ''Jonas...''

In the next instant he caught her to him to begin the oldest ritual of all. Two bodies merged, two hearts soared as one far beyond the chickee and over the timelessness of the Glades, which had brought them together in the beginning, and would always be a part of their future.

HARLEQUIN
Romance®

This May, travel to Egypt with Harlequin Romance's FIRST
CLASS title #3126, A FIRST TIME FOR EVERYTHING by
Jessica Steele.

A little excitement was what she wanted. So Josslyn's sudden
assignment to Egypt came as a delightful surprise. Pity she
couldn't say the same about her new boss.

Thane Addison was an overbearing, domineering slave driver.
And yet sometimes Joss got a glimpse of an entirely different
sort of personality beneath his arrogant exterior. It was
enough that Joss knew despite having to work for this brute of
a man, she wanted to stay.

Not that Thane seemed to care at all what his temporary
secretary thought about him....

HARLEQUIN
American Romance®

THE ROMANCE THAT STARTED IT ALL!

For Diane Bauer and Nick Granatelli, the walk down the aisle was a rocky road....

Don't miss the romantic prequel to WITH THIS RING—

I THEE WED
BY ANNE McALLISTER

Harlequin American Romance #387

Let Anne McAllister take you to Cambridge, Massachusetts, to the night when an innocent blind date brought a reluctant Diane Bauer and Nick Granatelli together. For Diane, a smoldering attraction like theirs had only one fate, one future—marriage. The hard part, she learned, was convincing her intended....

Watch for Anne McAllister's I THEE WED, available *now* from Harlequin American Romance.

ITW

HARLEQUIN'S WISHBOOK
SWEEPSTAKES RULES & REGULATIONS
NO PURCHASE NECESSARY TO ENTER OR RECEIVE A PRIZE

1. To enter the Sweepstakes and join the Reader Service, affix the Four Free Books and Free Gifts sticker along with both of your Sweepstakes stickers to the Sweepstakes Entry Form. If you do not wish to take advantage of our Reader Service, but wish to enter the Sweepstakes only, do not affix the Four Free Books and Free Gifts sticker; affix only the Sweepstakes stickers to the Sweepstakes Entry Form. Incomplete and/or inaccurate entries are ineligible for that section or sections of prizes. Torstar Corp. and its affiliates are not responsible for mutilated or unreadable entries or inadvertent printing errors. Mechanically reproduced entries are null and void.

2. Whether you take advantage of this offer or not, on or about April 30, 1992 at the offices of Marden-Kane Inc., Lake Success, NY, your Sweepstakes number will be compared against a list of winning numbers generated at random by the computer. However, prizes will only be awarded to individuals who have entered the Sweepstakes. In the event that all prizes are not claimed, a random drawing will be held from all qualified entries received from March 30, 1990 to March 31, 1992, to award all unclaimed prizes. All cash prizes (Grand to Sixth), will be mailed to the winners and are payable by check in U.S. funds. Seventh prize to be shipped to winners via third-class mail. These prizes are in addition to any free, surprise or mystery gifts that might be offered. Versions of this sweepstakes with different prizes of approximate equal value may appear in other mailings or at retail outlets by Torstar Corp. and its affiliates.

3. The following prizes are awarded in this sweepstakes: ★ Grand Prize (1) $1,000,000; First Prize (1) $25,000; Second Prize (1) $10,000; Third Prize (5) $5,000; Fourth Prize (10) $1,000; Fifth Prize (100) $250; Sixth Prize (2,500) $10; ★ ★ Seventh Prize (6,000) $12.95 ARV.

   ★ This Sweepstakes contains a Grand Prize offering of a $1,000,000 annuity. Winner will receive $33,333.33 a year for 30 years without interest totalling $1,000,000.

   ★ ★ Seventh Prize: A fully illustrated hardcover book published by Torstar Corp. Approximate Retail Value of the book is $12.95.

   Entrants may cancel the Reader Service at anytime without cost or obligation to buy (see details in center insert card).

4. Extra Bonus! This presentation offers two extra bonus prizes valued at a total of $33,000 to be awarded in a random drawing from all qualified entries received by March 31, 1992. No purchase necessary to enter or receive a prize. To qualify, see instructions on the insert card. Winner will have the choice of merchandise offered or a $33,000 check payable in U.S. funds. All other published rules and regulations apply.

5. This Sweepstakes is being conducted under the supervision of Marden-Kane, Inc., an independent judging organization. By entering this Sweepstakes, each entrant accepts and agrees to be bound by these rules and the decisions of the judges, which shall be final and binding. Odds of winning in the random drawing are dependent upon the total number of entries received. Taxes, if any, are the sole responsibility of the winners. Prizes are nontransferable. All entries must be received at the address printed on the reply card and must be postmarked no later than 12:00 MIDNIGHT on March 31, 1992. The drawing for all unclaimed Sweepstakes prizes and for the Bonus Sweepstakes Prize will take place May 30, 1992, at 12:00 NOON at the offices of Marden-Kane, Inc., Lake Success, NY.

6. This offer is open to residents of the U.S., the United Kingdom, France and Canada, 18 years or older, except employees and their immediate family members of Torstar Corp., its affiliates, subsidiaries, and all other agencies and persons connected with the use, marketing or conduct of this Sweepstakes. All Federal, State, Provincial and local laws apply. Void wherever prohibited or restricted by law. Any litigation within the Province of Quebec respecting the conduct and awarding of a prize in this publicity contest must be submitted to the Régie des Loteries et Courses du Québec.

7. Winners will be notified by mail and may be required to execute an affidavit of eligibility and release, which must be returned within 14 days after notification or an alternative winner may be selected. Canadian winners will be required to correctly answer an arithmetical skill-testing question administered by mail, which must be returned within a limited time. Winners consent to the use of their names, photographs and/or likenesses for advertising and publicity in conjunction with this and similar promotions without additional compensation.

8. For a list of major winners, send a stamped, self-addressed envelope to: WINNERS LIST, c/o MARDEN-KANE, INC., P.O. BOX 701, SAYREVILLE, NJ 08871. Winners Lists will be fulfilled after the May 30, 1992 drawing date.

ALTERNATE MEANS OF ENTRY: Print your name and address on a 3″ × 5″ piece of plain paper and send to:

In the U.S.
Harlequin's WISHBOOK Sweepstakes
3010 Walden Ave.
P.O. Box 1867, Buffalo, NY 14269-1867

In Canada
Harlequin's WISHBOOK Sweepstakes
P.O. Box 609
Fort Erie, Ontario L2A 5X3

LTY-H491RRD

HARLEQUIN Temptation

Lovers Apart